BRIDE FOR THE DEPUTY

Mail Order Brides of Christmas Mountain, Book 2

JO GRAFFORD, WRITING AS JOVIE GRACE

ISBN: 978-1-944794-89-7

GET A FREE BOOK!

Join my mailing list to be the first to know about new releases, free books, special discount prices, Bonus Content, and giveaways.

https://BookHip.com/GNVABPD

CHAPTER 1: BETROTHAL SCHEMES

JESSE

May, 1892 — La Casa foothills, Texas

I *wasn't born with a silver spoon in my mouth. Not even close!*

But Edward Remington had been. And, because of it, Jesse Hawling secretly despised him. It wasn't that Edward was a bad fellow, because he wasn't. He was actually a pretty even-tempered, charitable minded, law-abiding citizen — one of those nauseating do-gooders. Jesse simply despised him on principle, because nothing more than happenstance had caused Edward to step into this world, surrounded by wealth, while Jesse had been raised as poor as a church mouse.

He tried not to think about how thin the soles of his boots were, as he strode down the dusty streets of downtown La Casa. Or how threadbare his shirt was. Or how many times his denim trousers had been patched. Or even the fact that he could finally afford to replace all three of them, if he chose to. His position as the newest deputy at the sheriff's office paid a decent wage.

But his new wardrobe would have to wait. His mind was

made up. Deputy Jesse Hawling was going to fork out the money for a mail-order bride, instead. He reached the adobe storefront he was seeking, twisted the doorknob, and let himself inside.

Clink Redwood glanced up from his desk in the center of the room. Eyeing Jesse with interest, he spoke around the cigar he was puffing on. "Wondered which one of you Hawling boys was gonna be the first to pay me a visit." Even sitting down, he was a tall, thin creature — all sharp angles from his hooked nose to his pointy elbows. He puffed out a trio of perfect white smoke rings while he waited for an answer.

Jesse glanced around the sparsely furnished office. According to the growing line of prospective grooms in town, the new mail-order bride agency was like a ray of sunlight shining in a dark corner — a magical company that would usher lovely ladies into their all-male world. What Jesse saw, however, was a row of mismatched coffee mugs on an uneven desk. Folders brimming with bridal applications were stacked on each corner like papery anchors. It didn't appear that Mr. Redwood had done much more than hang his shingle outside and go to work. There were no paintings on the wall, no picture frames displayed on his desk, and no spare chair in which a visitor might park himself and stay a spell.

"I've been watching and waiting," Jesse announced airily. He stuffed his hands in his pockets and paced the nearly empty room, whistling softly beneath his breath.

"For what?" Mr. Redwood inquired dryly.

Jesse glanced out the front picture window to the dusty Main Street beyond. "Results, for one thing." Out of the corner of his eye, he watched Mr. Redwood's shoulders stiffen defensively. "Haven't seen you match too many brides and grooms yet. In fact, I can only recall one successful match. Edward Remington, I believe?" He spun swiftly in the matchmaker's direction. "Why haven't you married off more of our men in town?"

"Now, Jesse!" Mr. Redwood chided in a mild voice. "You know as well as I do that a bunch of my gentlemen customers aren't yet paid in full for my services. I cain't rightly move forward with my end of the bargain before they move forward with their end."

Can but won't. "Have you ever considered finding them wives with a bit of coin to their name?" he shot back. "Seems to me you'd get paid quicker if you did."

Mr. Redwood abruptly withdrew his cigar from his mouth. "That's not how this business works."

This business. Jesse couldn't think of a less romantic way of describing a mail-order bride service. If he hadn't walked through the door, predisposed to sign a contract, nothing Mr. Redwood had said so far would've convinced him to do so.

"Well, I'd prefer a wealthy wife," Jesse drawled, thoroughly enjoying the matchmaker's discomfort, "so much so that I plan to put my request in writing. However, I might be willing to compromise on the money issue if you'd agree to find me a high-born lady, instead."

"That's a ridiculous request!" Mr. Redwood recoiled, clearly insulted at being told how to run his business.

Jesse continued as if he hadn't heard the fellow. "She can be an impoverished gentlewoman, who's fallen on hard times. Or, perhaps, a spirited debutante involved in such a wicked scandal that her family cannot wait to unload her on the first poor, unsuspecting soul who crosses her path." He went on to describe a few more titillating scenarios in which Mr. Redwood might consider peddling his matchmaking wares to the upper-crust of society.

Mr. Redwood jammed his cigar back in his mouth and gnashed it between his teeth, probably wishing it was one of Jesse's fingers he was gnawing on. "My clientele are impoverished, and I've yet to see any of them brandishing a pedigree to go along with their lack of substance. In my experience, most poor folks start off that way and stay that way."

"Though you've yet to run across a rich mail-order bride, I'd argue it is still possible," Jesse countered slyly.

"Theoretically," the matchmaker grumbled, "but not the least bit likely."

"Would you be willing to search harder for a rich bride if I promise to pay double your regular fees?"

Clink Redwood's gaze turned hungry. He smoothed a hand through his thinning white hair and opened his mouth to speak.

"Half now and half later," Jesse interjected quickly. "It'll be like paying one hundred percent up front for one of your regular bridal contracts. Seeing as how forking over the money is the only way to get you working on the match-making part of the deal, correct?"

"Yes, but—"

"Good." Jesse reached inside the pocket of his denim trousers to withdraw a small wad of bills. He proceeded to whip off one bill at a time, silently counting each one. However, he mostly did it to watch Mr. Redwood salivate. "Where do I sign?"

Mr. Redwood's eyes bulged in sheer mesmerization, while Jesse continued peeling off dollar bills. "Like I said, there aren't exactly any guarantees in this business."

Jesse paused in his counting, pretending to be disappointed. "Well, you can't rightly expect me to pay double your regular fees, if you're just planning on pocketing my money and walking away." He lowered his fistful of money toward his pocket. "I certainly had higher hopes than that."

"Wait!" Mr. Redwood licked his dry lips, looking desperate. "I'll do my best to find you a well-heeled wife. I truly will, but it might take some time."

"Fortunately for both of us, time is something I have plenty of." Jesse was only two and twenty years old, and he actually wasn't all that interested in getting himself hitched to a perfect stranger any time soon. What he was interested in was acquiring wealth. And it seemed to him that signing one of Clink Redwood's mail-order bride contracts was a gamble worth taking in that direction.

"So we have a deal?" he inquired in a low voice, as he brandished his wad of dollar bills once again.

"I reckon we do." Mr. Redwood's voice was infused with a dozen reservations as he hastily wrote out the details of their arrangement on one of his agency contracts. Then he spun the document around on his desk so that Jesse could see what he'd written. "If you'll just sign here." He pointed. "And here." His gaze kept drifting back to the money in Jesse's hand.

Yes, indeed, money still talks. Jesse liked the fact that he was finally the one brandishing some of it. Clink's contracts didn't run cheap, so it had taken Jesse many months to save such a lofty sum. Never before had he felt so powerful.

More than anything, he liked the status it would afford him. If Clink Redwood succeeded in finding Jesse what he was asking for, his new bride would be better connected socially than even Edward Remington's wife. And as far as Jesse was concerned, the classier and snootier his future bride was, the better. Though Edward's wife, Lacey, was sweet-tempered, and the nephew she was raising was as cute as a button, her only claim to wealth was the fact that she'd married into wealth. He saw no reason why a fellow like him couldn't do the same.

Then, and only then, would the Hawlings' desperate cycle of poverty finally be broken. And if Jesse happened to be in the position to lord that fact over a highfalutin' Remington, he'd be that much happier!

"I CANNOT BELIEVE MY GUARDIAN IS BLAMING ME FOR failing to bring your brother up to scratch." Though Iris Hildebrand kept her voice carefully controlled, she was inwardly seething with indignation. She smoothed her hands down the skirt of her lavender day gown, trying to tamp down on her agitation. How dare the blasted man take her so thoroughly to task for something outside of her control! She was still smarting from the tongue-lashing he'd delivered to her an hour earlier.

"I reckon he was beside himself with disappointment. Surely you are aware that allying our families by marriage was a plan more than twenty years in the making." Richard Remington, the older brother of her former affianced, patted her arm comfortingly. "Just give your uncle a little more time, and he'll come up with the right solution to our current dilemma. You'll see."

Richard's easy acceptance of the scandal his younger brother had caused made her lips part in shock. They were strolling through the courtyard outside her childhood home, a once lovely rose garden that was quickly becoming choked with weeds. Her guardian and uncle, Fargus Hildebrand, had arrived at the estate a mere three months ago. However, he'd made a plethora of drastic changes during that time, not the least of which was terminating the employment of the entire landscaping crew.

"I wish I shared your confidence," she muttered, no longer trying to hide her bitterness. *And your position of strength.* Now that Edward had been disowned by the Remingtons, Richard was the sole heir to the family fortune. Not to mention, he was a man. He had a say in things. His opinions mattered. Iris, on the other hand, was at the mercy of the whims of her last living male relative.

"Speaking of wishes," Richard said quietly. "If it were possible, I'd marry you myself. Alas, my hand is already spoken for."

"You wish to marry me?" Iris blinked and missed a step. That was certainly news to her. "Truly?" Oh, if only such a thing were possible! Come to think of it, marrying Richard would be the perfect solution to her troubles.

"Of course." Grinning, Richard clasped her arm more tightly to help her regain her balance. "We've known each other for years. I think we'd rub along famously."

Rub along? Iris couldn't think of a less romantic-sounding expression. Though she knew he was only trying to cheer her up, she had no interest in marrying a man that she would simply *rub along* with. All her life, she'd secretly dreamed of more. Even when it came to her arranged marriage with Edward, she'd imagined them falling in love some day and finding happiness together.

Oh, Edward! How could you do this to me? She'd been under the mistaken impression that she and her former affianced were friends, at least. Yet he'd gone and done the unthinkable. Not only was he in breach of the marriage contract her father had arranged for them — may the dear soul rest in peace — Edward had irrevocably besmirched his good family name by pledging his hand to some moneyless, title-less mail-order bride.

It was a scandal of epic proportions, one that was currently raging like a storm through the uppermost levels of New York society. Iris couldn't step outside the gates of her home without being swamped by varying measures of gossip, speculation, and pity. Her ears were ringing with the phrases "left at the altar" and "the stain of rejection."

In some ways, the worst part of her humiliation was the fact that she'd had the misfortune to meet "the other woman in Edward's life" a few weeks ago during a trip out west.

Edward's parents, Penn and Alda Remington, had insisted on dragging Iris along in their fruitless journey. They hoped her presence would somehow jolt their wayward son "back to his senses." There was only one problem with their theory; they'd discovered Edward enjoying the undeniable state of married bliss.

"What are we doing, Richard?" Iris demanded so suddenly that his steps ground to a halt beneath the next rose trellis.

"What are we doing, you ask?" His kind, dark eyes regarded her quizzically. "I specifically recall you agreeing to a stroll in the courtyard." His mouth quirked. "My plan was to offer comfort, though it is clear I am failing miserably."

"Not that," she snapped, shaking off his arm. She waved her hands in the air. "I simply can't help wondering if Edward has the right of it. You weren't there in Texas when we paid him a visit, so you'll just have to take my word for it, but he actually seemed happy on that blasted mountain of his!"

"Why, Iris!" When Richard reached for her shoulders, she backed away a few steps.

"Don't *Why, Iris!* me," she retorted. "I truly want to know if you think we are doing what is right by following the dictates of our elders like meek little lambs."

Richard had to be aware that an irate Fargus Hildebrand was inside her late father's office right this minute with Penn Remington, spinning yet more mayhem with her future. There was no way it was merely a business meeting between a client and his lawyer — not while Richard was outside strolling through the gardens with Iris. If the two men had been inside discussing a routine legal matter, Richard would've been included. And who in tarnation was the shriveled old peanut who'd been driven to the front door of her home an hour earlier in a gold-gilded carriage? King Midas?

A shiver of alarm worked its way up Iris's spine as the details of a whole new theory formed in her mind. Richard's troubled gaze wasn't helping to alleviate her fears one bit, either. He hadn't so much as flinched at her earlier outburst. It was almost as if... She turned to him with a gasp of realization. He'd been expecting it!

"Richard!" She backed away from him in burgeoning horror. "You know what's going on inside my home, do you not?" She pointed a shaking finger in the direction of her father's office window. It overlooked the rear grounds of her family estate, so it was in plain view of the gardens where they were walking.

"Now, Iris," he cajoled. "There's no reason to get so worked up about—"

"You know what's going on, because you're a part of it," she continued sourly. "All of you are." She glanced in trepidation across the courtyard. Her cousin was sitting on a swing about twenty feet away, pretending to read a book.

Camille was Fargus Hildebrand's only daughter. Despite the fact that she and her father were Iris's last living kin, however, she barely knew either of them. Her father had not been close with his only brother. In fact, she could only recall the man visiting on one other occasion — for her mother's funeral eight years earlier.

"Oh, give way!" Camille cried impatiently, glancing up at last from her book. She was a doll-like creature with long, golden curls draping the shoulders of her pale pink gown. "Of course we are all gathered here today because of you. The scandal you've caused is affecting us all. If Father allowed it to run rampant much longer, we'd all be doomed to a future as social outcasts."

Iris was aghast. "How could you say such a thing, my dear cousin? It's not as if I did anything wrong." She'd respected her parents and followed their guidance her entire life. Because of them, she could dance like a fairy and sing like an angel. Because of them, she knew how to speak French and could paint the most glorious watercolors. They'd spared no expense in ensuring she had the finest tutors at her disposal.

"Nothing wrong?" Camille stood and shook an imaginary wrinkle from her lacy skirts. "Well, you certainly did nothing right, either. It's obvious you haven't heard the worst of the rumors. Half of New York is now claiming that Edward fled from the notion of being bound for all eternity to a woman with such a horrible affliction."

"What affliction?" Iris cried. "I have no affliction." Other than the misfortune of being saddled with such a scheming, greedy guardian. A man who hadn't wanted a thing to do with his niece her entire life, yet hadn't hesitated to come scrambling like a roach out of the woodwork to manage her vast fortune after her father's death.

"Does it matter?" Camille returned. "The end result is the same. Your failure to wed Edward has done irrevocable harm to the Hildebrand name. And, unlike yourself, I've no intention of sitting here idly and being rendered unmarriageable."

"Unmarriageable?" Iris squeaked, hardly able to believe what she was hearing.

"Well, maybe not entirely." Camille's smile was brimming with malice. "You did receive one last respectable offer of marriage. Granted, he's getting up there in years, but there are many women who still consider Rafe Blackbourne to be quite the romantic figure."

For a moment, Iris thought she might faint. No wonder the family crest on the gold gilded carriage parked out front seemed vaguely familiar. Though she'd never been personally introduced to Rafe Blackbourne, he was known far and wide for his rakish ways. He'd buried three or four wives already and had sired an astronomical number of children among them. It was no wonder the pitiful women had chosen the grave over remaining topside with his lascivious self.

"Now, Camille!" Richard chided as he reached for Iris's elbow. "Is that any way to treat a grieving cousin?"

Iris could hardly believe his persistence in treating her like a helpless ninny. Yes, she was grieving the loss of her father, but grief wasn't driving her current set of emotions. Rage was!

"I will not marry Mr. Blackbourne." Her voice was coldly final as she turned her back on her audience and drew in a bracing breath of air. The man in question was more than twice her age. Not to mention a lecher of the worst sort. She was certain her father would never have made such a callus and unfair demand of her, if he was still alive.

"I am sorry that Edward's failure to honor our marriage contract has caused our family so much trouble," she continued in the same crisp tone, "but there has to be a better way to fix this."

"There's not." Camille's voice was falsely cheerful.

"Then your father isn't trying hard enough." Iris's mind was made up. If Uncle Fargus truly thought he could get away with wedding his only niece to the aging Rafe Blackbourne, then she'd just have to hire a lawyer of her own to fight him. She possessed a generous monthly allowance in which to do so. "I've a good mind to tell him so myself." Speaking her mind at last was both thrilling and terrifying. She'd never done anything so bold in all her days.

She moved forward with purpose before she lost her nerve. However, Richard jogged around her to plant himself directly in front of her, blocking her path. "As your friend, I do not advise you to say or do anything hasty, my dear."

She tried to brush past him, but he gripped her elbows, forcing her to look up at him.

She raised her chin. "A friend would not have spent the past half hour pretending like nothing was wrong. A friend would have warned me that a plot was afoot to destroy my happiness."

Disappointment made his dark brows furrow. "You sound as if you've been reading those infernal novels again."

His accusation made her blush to the roots of her white-blonde hair. How dare he make her occasional escape to the world of fiction sound like something so dark and sordid? Heaven knew she had precious little else to look forward to!

"And if I have?" she taunted.

He dropped his voice to such a low tone that Camille most likely could not hear their conversation. "Then I pity you, because what is happening here today is not simply another chapter in one of your silly books. Your family legacy is at stake, Iris."

"My father's fortune, you mean." She gritted her teeth at his condescending tone.

"That's part of it, too. Suffice to say, a great number of people have a vested interest in your future. That's just the way of the world, my angry little friend."

"A fancy way of saying that I'm nothing more than a bargaining chip." Iris felt her earlier burst of confidence start to crumble.

"I disagree, but methinks you're far too distraught to hear any more of my opinions on the topic today."

"Oh, *now* you wish to write me off as some distraught female," she rasped, feeling her face pale. "Has our friendship really come to this?"

"Iris, my love!" a deep male voice boomed from behind them.

She flinched at the inexplicable glee in her uncle's voice. His anger from earlier was gone. In its place was an emotion that was difficult for her to describe. She sensed a restless brand of triumph in him, a tightly-wound anticipation.

Richard gave her elbows one last squeeze before letting

her go. She slowly spun to face her guardian. "What is it, Uncle Fargus?"

"I have good news," he breezed, striding in her direction with his arms outstretched. "You're to be married at last, my precious niece."

An older man wearing a black suit, plenty of wrinkles around his eyes, and a knowing leer, followed in his wake.

"To whom?" she inquired stiffly.

His smile dimmed a few degrees. "To one of New York's finest gentlemen. I couldn't be more honored to introduce you to Mr. Rafe Blackbourne, your groom-to-be."

Iris's insides turned icy. "He most certainly is not!" she gasped. So great was her shock at her uncle's announcement that the words slipped out before she could give them any further consideration.

Her uncle's expression turned thunderous. "Of all the ingratitude!" he snarled. "I confess I'm running vastly short of patience with your lack of ladylike decorum. Your father must be rolling over in his grave right now."

"I tried to warn you," Richard muttered from somewhere nearby.

Iris waved a trembling hand in a vain attempt to wipe away his words. "If my father's peace has been disturbed, it is by your own highhandedness, Uncle Fargus. Marching into our home with your greedy, grasping ways. Be assured you'll be hearing from my attorney in short order. Good day, gentlemen." Raising her head high, she sailed from the courtyard, not daring to look back.

"Such spirit," her would-be fiancé chortled. His voice grew stern with warning. "Like that of a wild filly, it will be broken, I assure you."

Iris had no doubt his words were intended to carry to her. By now, she was trembling so badly it was difficult to continue putting one foot in front of the other. The last thing she heard before stepping inside the rear entrance of the mansion was Camille's snide voice.

"I fear she's worse off than any of us ever imagined. She's been talking out of her head the whole time we were out here."

With a low moan of misery, Iris made her way through the dim hallways of her home, only distantly registering how dusty it had become since her uncle's arrival. She dragged her weary limbs up the long, curving stairwell to the second floor and made her way to her private suite of rooms. Behind the closed doors of her inner sanctum, she would be able to breathe freely again for a few moments — long enough to compose herself and pack her bags for a proper exit. She'd pack a bag and leave before dark. There was no way she was spending even one more night beneath the same roof as her dastardly, conniving uncle.

Buoyed by the thought of her plans for a swift exit, Iris threw open the door of her bedchamber and stopped short.

A plump woman of uncertain years with an unreadable expression stood there. Her expectant stance indicated she'd been waiting for Iris.

"Hello, Miss Hildebrand." Her voice was just as bland as her expression. She was dressed in a gown of white cotton with a matching cap like that of a nurse. Even her lace-up boots were white.

Iris stared. "Who are you?" She glanced furtively over her shoulder, gauging the distance to the stairs in the event she needed to make a hasty retreat.

"Someone here to help you," the strange woman soothed.

"How? Did you know my father?" Iris wanted more than anything to believe that the good Lord had sent her an ally in her time of need. However, good sense wouldn't allow her to view the woman standing before her as anything more than an intruder until she identified herself.

"But of course, my dear. He knew things would be diffi-cult for you after he passed and—." Quick as a flash, the woman was upon her.

With one large, vise-like hand, she gripped Iris's upper arm. In the same moment, she plunged something sharp into Iris's neck.

"What are you doing?" Terror like she'd never known before lodged itself in Iris's throat. The woman's face wavered before her eyes. Then her bedchamber and everything in it disappeared, as she slipped toward oblivion.

CHAPTER 2: PARTNERS IN CRIME

JESSE

One week later

J esse fiddled with the papery summons from Clink Redwood. It amused him to no end that the aging matchmaker had sent him a message by way of a courier. Talk about going overboard with formalities! His words were brief and solidly to the point.

Found a prospective bride. More details at noon. My office.

Folding the note and stuffing it inside the pocket of his leather vest, Jesse started to whistle as he skipped down the stairs of his apartment over the jailhouse. Technically, the upstairs loft was only a place to nap when work became so demanding that it was necessary to pull an overnight shift. Since Jesse and his brother's lived halfway up Christmas Mountain, however, he'd gotten into the habit of using the loft apartment a bit more often — especially on the coldest, rainiest, or snowiest nights. He'd even negotiated a deal with the livery down the street. That way he could board his Palomino nearby on the nights he chose to stay in town.

"You look mighty cheerful today." Sheriff Rick Dawson

glanced up from his newly constructed pine desk at the front of the office. He pierced Jesse with his all-seeing gray gaze. "Any chance it means you caught a break in our latest horse rustling case?"

A month earlier, the sheriff had commissioned Jonah, Jesse's oldest brother, to replace nearly every stick of furniture in the station. Jesse couldn't help noting the proud way the sheriff had both hands resting on his desktop, clearly admiring it. And the way he was seated in his matching high-back chair inevitably brought to mind a king on his throne. If Jonah took on a few more construction projects like this, he would be slapping some serious coin in the bank. Yes, indeed, the Hawling brothers were moving up in the world!

"No break on our case yet, Sheriff, but you can rest assured I'll remain on the lookout for clues, even tomorrow on my day off." Jesse figured a gentle reminder was in order, since his boss pretty much acted like they were never off duty. He was only five or six years older than Jesse, but he might as well have been twenty years older with the way he lorded his position of authority over him.

"I appreciate your diligence on the case, Deputy Hawling." His boss sounded amused. "You look like you're on your way out the door. Where might you be heading?"

Oh, joy! Here comes his mile-long list of last-minute tasks. Jesse carefully schooled his expression to one of polite attentiveness, though he inwardly braced himself to be sorely inconvenienced. "Out to lunch," he answered vaguely.

"I don't reckon your lunch plans will take you anywhere near the post office?" The sheriff sounded moderately distracted as he bent his head to peer more closely at the map spread across his desk. He had to shove back a shock of auburn hair that fell across his eyes.

"It might. Do you want me to pick up the mail?" There was no point in playing the fool. When it came to the sheriff's long list of chores, it was generally a matter of volunteering or being volunteered.

"I'd be much obliged if you did." By now, the sheriff both looked and sounded distracted. "And if you happen to be near the post office, that'll also put you near the General Store." By the time he finished mumbling over his map, Jesse had been assigned a half dozen more places to visit, which would keep him dashing around town a good hour or two.

So much for his intention to return right after his appointment at the mail-order bride agency and immediately get back to work. Most of his afternoon would be spent trotting around and playing the part of Rick Dawson's errand boy. Fortunately, his boss had no way of knowing what order Jesse did his assigned tasks in.

Clapping on his well-worn brown leather Stetson, he made a bee-line for the livery first. Retrieving his horse, he trotted the main road winding its way up the mountain to the adobe storefront that housed the town's mail-order bride agency. It was still a fairly new enterprise, only a few months old.

Arriving at the tethering post, he canted his head upward, noting the presence of a few gathering clouds. No wonder it was beginning to look overcast. They were due for some rain. Though he drew a line at getting soaked straight to the skin, Jesse didn't mind the thought of a little rain. It had been an awfully dry and dusty spring, so far. A few inches of rainfall might be in order to hold the dirt in place. Then again, the rain clouds might just as easily roll straight past. The weather in this part of the country was, at best, unpredictable.

He pushed open the door to the agency and stepped inside. To his surprise, it was less smoky than usual. Even more surprising, Clink Redwood wasn't lounging at his desk. Instead, he was pacing the back wall of the room so energetically, it was a wonder he wasn't wearing a hole in the plank flooring. Or in the soles of his new shiny black leather boots.

Putting my bridal contract fees to good use already, eh? Jesse hid a grin as he demanded, "Well? What's the news about my bride?" There was no point in mincing words, since the two of them had the office to themselves.

Clink rounded on him with a gusty expulsion. "How about I start off with a confession?"

Jesse grimaced at the possibility that the old matchmaker had stretched the truth in his message. It certainly didn't appear that he had a woman stowed away anywhere in his office.

"There's a part of me that's hollering we should stay as far from this particular woman as possible," Clink continued in a strained voice, "but a deal is a deal. In exchange for your money, I gave you my word that I'd do everything in my power to hunt you down a rich wife." He paused, rubbing his chin and looking a good ten shades of agitated.

"And?" Jesse prodded.

"I think I found a prospect for you," the older fellow declared in a mournful tone.

Jesse straightened, wondering what had the matchmaker's face all pinched with distress. "You don't sound too excited over that fact."

"I'm not." Clink moved behind his desk to shuffle a few folders of papers around.

"Why not? So long as you hold up your end of our bargain, you have another payday coming. A generous one. Seems to me that should be a cause for celebrating."

Clink kept talking as if he hadn't heard Jesse. "I was shocked to receive her telegram, seeing as New York was not one of the cities I advertised in. I was planning on it, of course. Just hadn't gotten around to it yet."

"New York, you say?" Jesse's ears perked at the name. It

was where the innkeeper of Christmas Mountain was from, the man who just so happened to employ both of his brothers. The same man whom Jesse felt as if he was constantly competing with.

"Yes. I reckon, by some round about way, she might've gotten wind of your advertisement for a bride from a friend or family member." Clink scratched his head. "There has to be an explanation."

"So there's a woman in New York who wants to marry me, eh?" Jesse rocked back on his heels, feeling smug.

"Believe me, I'm as surprised as you are. Unless I'm mistaken, she's the same high and mighty chit from back east who was supposed to marry Edward Remington."

Come again? Jesse, who'd not until that very moment felt any of the surprise that the matchmaker seemed to think he should be experiencing, rounded on the man with his jaw falling open. "Are you, by any chance, referring to Iris Hildebrand?" What were the odds?

"I am." Clink's silvery gaze clashed with his and held. "I take it, you've met her?"

I most certainly have! "I reckon you could say that." Jesse resisted the urge to chuckle as he recalled the hissing young beauty who'd attempted to stare down her perfect nose at him. In the next moment, he'd caught her mid-air, when her boots went flying out from beneath her on the icy porch stairs. She'd all but dissolved into tears in his arms. That was when he'd realized how much of her previous hauteur had been for show. She was valiantly struggling to avoid becoming completely unraveled, and it was all Edward Remington's fault.

The innkeeper had once been her affianced, promised to her by an arranged marriage between their two wealthy families. To this day, Jesse wasn't entirely certain what had gone wrong with the engagement. All he knew was that Edward had failed to honor it. *The cad!* Instead, he'd sent off for a mail-order bride and married the first woman Clink Redwood had sent his way, Lacey Cleveland. The fetching inn proprietress was now Lacey Remington, and the two of them showed every sign of being happy together. *Good gravy!* Even when Edward Remington screwed something up, it had a way of working out easy as pie for him!

"Well?" Clink Redwood brusquely interrupted Jesse's reverie. "You said you've already met her. Was it amicable?"

"It's complicated." Jesse smirked, recalling how good it felt to have Iris's delicate frame nestled in his embrace. His heart always twisted a bit at the memory of what happened next. He'd replayed her hastily whispered apology in his head again and again, and could come up with only one explanation for the way she'd proceeded to shriek at him like a banshee to unhand her, right before she delivered a stinging slap to his cheek. *Women!* They'd been driving men to the brink of insanity for centuries.

"How complicated?" The furrow in Clink's brow deepened. "I'm trying to figure out just how much work we have ahead of us, and if this woman is even worth your time pursuing."

"She's worth it," Jesse growled, surprising both of them with his quick defense of her.

"Do tell," Clink declared mildly, looking fascinated.

"How about you just keep talking?" Jesse countered. He had no interest in sharing the intimate details of their first encounter. "What exactly did Iris Hildebrand say in her telegram?" More than anything, he was burning to know why in tarnation a woman of her tremendous wealth would ever stoop to signing a mail-order bride contract.

Clink shrugged. "She didn't say much, only that she was already on her way to Christmas Mountain and that you were to meet her at the stagecoach stop tomorrow morning."

"To marry me?" Jesse asked carefully, still not ready to believe it. There had to be more to the story.

"That's what she said. Oh, and she specifically stated she was not traveling alone. I can only presume that means she's traveling with a ladies' companion or servant." He jammed his long, bony hands in his pockets and started pacing again. "Normally, I would be the one to go fetch my clients, but since she specifically requested you..." He allowed his words to dwindle on a suggestive note.

"I'll go meet her," Jesse assured quickly.

"Fine, but be sure to bring her right back here. Pronto." Clink gave a decided nod. "There's still paperwork to be signed, the marriage ceremony to arrange, and so forth."

"Understood." Jesse wasn't so certain there would be a forthcoming marriage ceremony. Regardless of Iris Hildebrand's reasons for suddenly wanting to become a mail-order bride, there was no way she'd choose to come to Christmas Mountain of all places in the country — the hometown of the man who'd jilted her. It simply didn't add up.

So if she hadn't chosen to come, the other possibility was that she was being forced to travel here. He mulled over the details of her journey. There was something singularly odd about her insistence on meeting him at the stagecoach stop, as well as her deliberate mention of the fact she was not alone. Come to think of it, a woman of her vast financial resources shouldn't be traveling by way of a public stagecoach at all, with or without a companion. Jesse's deputy mind swiftly processed the details of the situation and could only come up with one truly viable conclusion.

Iris Hildebrand was in some sort of trouble. It might not hurt to send a telegram to the sheriff's department in New York City and do a little old-school detective work on her behalf. It wasn't the horse rustling case he was supposed to be working on, but Jesse's gut told him it was the one and only case he should be focusing his attention on at the moment.

ONE DAY LATER

Iris sluggishly pushed herself upright against the hard, unforgiving stagecoach seat. *Mercy!* Every inch of her body was sore from traveling. She and her captor had exited their train nearly two hours earlier on the side of some sagebrush-speckled canyon. From there, they'd boarded a dusty stage-coach that creaked and groaned with each turn of its wheels. They were currently jostling around its blasted cabin with four other passengers, all construction workers. It was as if their driver was trying to hit every rock, root, and rut between the train station and her final destination — the asylum.

She shivered at the memory of reading the name of the horrific place on the side of one of her many pill bottles, The West Texas Asylum. It was only by sheer happenstance she'd seen it. Or maybe it was due to her persistence in acting the part of the spoiled socialite for the duration of their trip. The result was that her captor, or ladies' companion as Miranda insisted on calling herself, had let down her guard in slow degrees.

She'd even attempted to explain away their first encounter, during which Iris had been forcefully medicated and removed from her home, claiming Iris had merely been given an "old remedy to calm one's nerves." Miranda had supposedly learned the technique from her mother, who was a nurse.

Hogwash! Iris was well aware, by now, that she'd been utterly betrayed by her evil uncle. She was being drugged and dragged across the country to an insane asylum, never to be seen or heard from again. She had no doubt that her uncle was right now attempting to claim to anyone who would listen that he'd removed her from her home for her own good — to cure her distraught state of mind following the death of her father or some other such nonsense.

She alone knew the sordid truth. Her uncle had no true sympathy for her plight of becoming an orphan, and he was not trying to cure her of anything. He was embroiled in a dubious and convoluted legal maneuver, in the attempt to gain complete and uncontested control over her fortune. And he had the assistance of none other than Penn Remington to pull it off. Edward's father. The same crusty old attorney who continued to blame her for his son's refusal to return to the family fold. It was the perfect crime, one that her uncle was likely to get away with, unless...

Despite her many bruised and stiff joints, Iris finished pulling herself into a sitting position, stifling a whimper of pain. "How soon until we arrive at my aunt's home?" she demanded.

"Soon, my dear." Though Miranda's mouth tightened at Iris's petulant tone, she'd long since determined it made her job easier to play along, which was all part of Iris's plan.

"Anytime this year?" Iris groused. "It seems to me that all we're doing is rattling our way from one dusty stop to another."

Miranda drew in a breath between gritted teeth. "There are only a few stops left, my dear. One coming up in an hour or so, and two more after that. If everything goes as planned, you'll be reunited with your aunt by dinner time."

Iris glanced drearily around the over-crammed cabin, hoping with all of her might that the events of the day would, in fact, *not* go as Miranda planned. *Please, Lord, let my message find its way to that cocky cowboy deputy.*

She couldn't help wondering if God even bothered

listening to the prayers of wealthy heiresses. If He did, however, He'd hopefully directed that grizzled little porter back on the train in New York to do what she'd paid him to do during one of those few, rare moments when Miranda wasn't supervising her. If so, her hastily recited message had been sent via a telegram to the mail-order bride agency that represented Jesse Hawling. It was only by chance she'd come across the discarded newspaper from Boston, advertising the fact that Deputy Jesse Hawling, of all people, was in the market for a bride.

Good gracious! She shivered at the thought of any woman joining hands with him at the altar. The man was barely civilized. However, he *was* a lawman. So if he received her desperate message and if he was foolish enough to believe she'd actually marry a man of his ilk, at least she'd have a deputy on the scene.

And that's where the toughest leap of faith was required. Even if her message was miraculously delivered into his dusty, callused hands, there was no guarantee he would have any interest in coming to the stagecoach stop to claim her as his bride. And why should he? She'd done nothing but insult and belittle him during their first encounter. Her cheeks burned all over again at the memory of the slap she'd delivered to his cheek.

"Are you feeling ill again, Miss Hildebrand?" her companion inquired slyly. "Your cheeks are flushed."

Iris bit her lower lip, knowing the woman was merely using her agitated state as an excuse to administer her next dose of sleeping pills. She rolled her eyes and pretended to wave away the pinkness in her cheeks. "Dear me, yes. My head aches without ceasing, and you continue to be all pinch-fisted with my medication." She took an unholy delight in the answering redness her words brought to her captor's cheeks.

"Here!" the woman snapped, whipping out the desired pill bottle and handing it over.

Grinning in false triumph, Iris shook a few extra pills than normal onto her palm. She tried not to shiver when her gaze fell again on the asylum's name printed on the side of the bottle.

"Why, Miss Hildebrand!" Miranda gasped, reaching for the bottle. "That's too many. If you take them all at once, they could make you ill."

Ha! As opposed to merely keeping me sedated? An interesting line for you to draw in the moral sand, madam! Iris pretended to pop two into her mouth, tipped back her head, and made a swallowing movement. Then she tucked all the pills into her reticule with the others she'd not taken for the last several days.

"For later." Iris treated her captor to a smug smile, daring her to contest her charge in front of the other passengers. "In the event you're asleep the next time I need a dose."

"Very well." Miranda gave a long-suffering sigh and glanced out the window, no doubt reminding herself that their difficult journey was nearly at an end.

Iris dipped her head forward to peer around Miranda at the endless stretches of hills and plains. *My lands!* A body could become lost in such a barren patch of countryside, never to be found again. A shiver of foreboding worked its way through her frame. No doubt that was exactly what her uncle was hoping would happen to her.

"Good gracious!" Miranda muttered, reaching up to touch Iris's forehead. "First you're hot, and now you're cold. I fear you may be catching a chill."

As if you'd care! It was all Iris could do not to call the woman out on her hypocrisy. *You're a truly wretched creature, accepting wages to kidnap an innocent woman. For shame!* However, Iris merely bit her lower lip again and tried to ignore the woman. She was still too busy contemplating how easy it would be for a person to disappear in such a craggy, mountainous region, including those who wanted to disappear.

Like herself.

Please, God. Her thoughts turned prayerful again. *Send that deputy to my rescue, and I'll turn over a new leaf. I'll stop taking my wealth for granted, and I'll spend the rest of my days doing good deeds.* Though Iris's parents had raised her to be charitable, she couldn't recall the last time she'd done something truly self-less. She'd gotten way too caught up in the whirl of her social life, and what good had it done her? *I'll feed the hungry. I'll sew garments for the poor. I'll make toys for the orphans. I'll do whatever You ask of me, Lord.*

Maybe her thoughts were nothing more than the ramblings of a desperate woman, but Iris felt better afterward.

"Ah," Miranda suddenly murmured. "We're almost at our next stop, my dear. I recognize that peak just ahead. The locals call it the praying beetle, because the rock formation looks exactly like an insect on its knees with its wings spread."

Iris wrinkled her nose, pretending distaste. "Ick. I deplore bugs. Pesky, disgusting creatures! All of them!"

Miranda gave her a sharp look, which served as a reminder that Iris was supposed to be growing sleepy from her most recent dose of medication.

She gave an affected yawn. "Somebody implore our snail of a driver to pick up his pace. I'm fast growing weary of traveling." Before she tipped her head back against the seat and closed her eyes, Iris cast one last furtive glance out the window. *Where are you, Deputy?*

To her surprise, a cloud of dust was billowing against the horizon in the distance. She watched it curiously, wondering if they were in for a dust storm. But, no. The cloud of dust remained hovering the same distance above the ground as it drew closer.

"Bandits!" one of the male passengers shouted in alarm. "Three of them, coming at us from the east!"

Bandits! Iris's heart thumped in alarm. She'd read about encounters like these, and they usually didn't end well. Sitting up and squinting out the window, she watched them approach with dread. The men on horses spread out as they drew closer, converging on the hapless stagecoach from three sides, closing off their only exit from the mountain pass.

The driver shouted epitaphs as he tugged on the horses' reins and brought them to a halt. Then he began the slow, painstaking process of turning the rig inside the narrow confines of the pass.

But there was no time. The bandits were already upon them. One rode the precariously narrow ledge above the stagecoach. The hooves of his beige Palomino rained pebbles down on them, peppering the roof of the stagecoach like hail.

One of Iris's fellow passengers produced a pistol and started shooting wildly in the direction of the horseman. Despite the fact that the bandit held a pair of pistols aimed in their direction, he did not shoot back. He sat there, still as death, allowing the barrels to glint like pure silver in the sunlight. His face was covered from the nose down with a dark kerchief, and his Stetson was pulled low over his eyes.

"Bloody outlaw is just out of shooting range," the angry passenger groaned. "We're sitting ducks!"

To Iris's surprise, a small derringer materialized in Miranda's hand, which she quickly leaned over and pressed into Iris's hand. "Shoot first, my dear, and ask questions later."

Iris blinked and tried to fake another yawn, despite the trepidation rolling through her.

"Enough!" Miranda snapped. She leaned closer to hiss directly in Iris's ear. "Our little game is ended, my dear. I've worked at the asylum long enough to recognize that you are neither insane as your uncle claimed, nor have you been properly sedated for the last few days as you pretended. The only reason I let you get away with the ruse was because it was better for both of us if you continued believing you were pulling the wool over my eyes."

Unsure what mischief Miranda was up to this time, Iris could only stare at the woman. "What do you want from me?" she rasped, no longer caring if the other passengers overheard her. If anything, their presence emboldened her.

"First and foremost, I want you to live." The woman's normally bland expression turned glassy with unshed tears. "I want you to survive whatever the highway robbers have planned for us. Then I want you to run for help. Find a sheriff and report everything that was wrongfully done to you by your uncle." She reached inside her pocket and withdrew a fistful of coins. "Here. Put these some place the robbers won't easily find."

Staring in amazement, Iris accepted the gift with trembling fingers and dropped them one-by-one inside her bodice. They settled against her flushed and feverish skin like a cool metal warning. "Why are you helping me?"

"Because I am in the business of collecting the insane, not the sane," Miranda sighed, "and I've known for days that you are sane. I just didn't quite know what to do about it. If I don't deliver you to the asylum, I could lose my job, you know."

Iris stared at her, aghast. *So you would sacrifice me to save yourself?* Surely the woman wasn't hoping to stir her pity, because Iris had none to spare for such a dastardly deed.

Three pistol shots echoed in rapid succession across the canyon, drawing her attention back to the window.

"You have something we want," the bandit on the beige Palomino called in a deep voice. "A young woman by the name of Iris Hildebrand. Have her step out alone with her hands raised, and the rest of you will be allowed to continue on. Deny our request, and none of you will leave the canyon alive."

The male passengers eyed the two women in varying degrees of speculation.

"He said he wanted the young one," the man sitting across from Iris muttered.

"No!" Miranda cried, looking horrified. "Do not even think of turning her out! She is in my care, and I'll not allow it."

"I don't like it any more than you do, ma'am," he cried, "but you heard the man. If we don't do as he says, we all die."

"He's probably bluffing." Miranda voice was tart, though it held a faint tremor of uncertainty.

Iris studied her drearily, knowing her former captor was too weak-willed to hold out for long against the opposition. If the situation came down to Miranda doing the right thing versus saving her own hide, Iris was fairly certain she knew what the woman's decision would be.

"What if he's not bluffing?" The man shuffled his work boots uncomfortably on the floor of the carriage. He seemed to be having trouble meeting her eyes.

"Bah!" another man growled. "It's a simple kidnapping, don't you see? Who's saying they mean the lass any harm at all? For all we know, they'll post a ransom to her rich family and be done with it." He nodded at Iris. "In case you haven't noticed, she ain't exactly dressed like the rest of us poor folk."

It was true. Iris's heart sank. She'd left New York in a designer dress of pale lavender silk. Though the underskirt was wrinkled from many days of travel, its many layers of finely woven lace remained a statement in refined elegance.

"I say we take a vote," a third man suggested in a low voice. "That way it's fair."

But there was nothing fair about the vote of four men against that of two helpless women, and everyone present knew it.

"You should be ashamed of what you are doing!" Miranda sobbed as the men threw open the stagecoach door and nudged Iris toward it.

"We are," the man closest to the door confessed as he assisted Iris to the ground.

She stood there, dazed and shaking, as the stagecoach slowly rolled away and picked up speed. Her two travel bags were still loaded on the roof, bearing all that remained of her earthly possessions. Only when the rig disappeared out the other end of the pass, did the bandits on horseback ride closer.

"Well, Miss Hildebrand," the man on the Palomino abruptly lowered the cloth from his face and let it settle around his neck. "I believe you summoned me?" His upper lip twisted sardonically. "Not, I suspect, to wed me as you claimed in your telegram to Mr. Redwood."

Jesse Hawling's mocking features swam into view, making Iris sway on her feet. "You came," she breathed. "You actually came." Alas, her knees chose that moment to give out, and she sank to the sandy ground.

CHAPTER 3: MONEY MATTERS

IRIS

I ris watched dizzily as her would-be savior pressed his knees to his horse's flanks to urge the creature forward.

"When a wealthy woman gives an order, a poor man jumps to do her bidding," he retorted dryly. Reaching her side, he held out a hand to her. "Expecting to be properly paid for his services, of course."

Right. Everything in her life always boiled down to money. For a moment, she tasted disappointment. Strange, how she'd expected Jesse Hawling to be different. Apparently, all men were money-grubbing fools. She stared at his callused hand, debating whether to take it. If she rested a minute or two longer, there was the distinct possibility she'd be able to summon the strength to rise to her feet unassisted.

"Aw, Jesse! Cut her some slack. Can't you see she's been through enough?" A tall, bear-like man rode closer to them, eyeing her in concern. His kerchief had also been lowered from his face and was now riding around his neck. Though his shoulders were broader and thicker than Jesse's, his coal black hair and coffee-colored eyes were too similar to be a coincidence.

"I'm Jonah, by the way." He grimaced at Jesse. "This bloke's brother. The oldest and wisest one."

A third, much thinner and wiry man rode into view, bearing the same black hair and assessing gaze. At Jonah's introduction, he gave a bark of laughter. "I'll agree to the oldest part, not so sure about the wisest, though." He gave Iris a friendly nod. "You probably don't remember me, but I'm Jack, the chef of Christmas Mountain Inn."

She nodded blankly, more than a little ashamed by the realization she did not, in fact, remember him. In the past, she'd been horribly guilty of ignoring the hired help, and her visit to the Christmas Mountain Inn a few months ago had been no exception.

"I'm Iris Hildebrand. Pleased to meet you," she murmured politely. She promised the good Lord in her many prayers over the last several days that she would turn over a new leaf, given the chance. Well, here was her chance — after they helped restore her to her rightful place in the world, of course.

Buoyed by the brothers' obvious sympathy for her plight, she struggled to find the right words to further rally their gallantry on her behalf. "And you're right, Deputy Hawling." Her gaze fluttered back to him. "I did not precisely come to Texas to marry you. It was quite by accident that I came across your mail-order bride advertisement at all." Feeling suddenly nervous beneath his piercing scrutiny, she hastened to explain. "It was printed in an out-of-town newspaper that someone else had discarded on the train."

He inclined his head to acknowledge her words. "If you do not intend to wed me, then what is it that you want from me, Miss Hildebrand?"

"Your help." Her face grew hot at the realization that Jesse Hawling wasn't looking or sounding nearly as uncivilized as she remembered.

He gave her a mocking bow. "How may I assist you, madam?"

There was no point in mincing words. Her situation was too desperate. "Though I don't plan to let him get away with it, my guardian took every last penny I owned, along with my home and everything in it. He additionally claimed I am not of a sound mind and deserved to be committed to an asylum. If you hadn't waylaid my coach, that was exactly where I was headed."

Jesse's expression didn't change, though his jaw hardened. "I figured you were in trouble. Couldn't think of many other reasons why a woman like you would respond to the bridal advertisement of a man like me."

She blinked in surprise, taken aback by the bitterness in his tone.

"What about the men on the coach?" he continued. "I counted four. Were they your captors?" He leaned down from his horse, waving his hand at her again and beckoning her to take it.

"No. Only the woman. Or so I thought." Iris closed her fingers around his much larger paw and allowed him to tug her to her feet. "Just before our fellow passengers took a vote to toss me out and leave me at your mercy, she made a very puzzling confession."

"Indeed?"

"She does not believe I am insane."

"Because you're not!" Jesse's voice was so sharply emphatic that she beheld him in amazement. "Here." He removed a canteen from his pack, uncapped it, and shoved it in her direction. "Drink."

In the past, she would've gotten all finicky over sharing a canteen with someone else, particularly someone of a lesser station in life, out of the fear of contracting some horrible plague. However, Iris was so thirsty that she immediately tipped it up and started drinking.

"Not too much too quickly," he warned. "Pace yourself."

The moment she handed his canteen back, Jesse offered his hand to her again. She took it, and he tugged her atop his horse.

Immediately, her insides were a-tremble for a whole new reason. She'd ridden side-saddle before, but never with a man riding behind her. And not just behind her. *My lands!* They were sitting flush against each other, with her right shoulder wedged securely against his chest and her full skirts draped across the knee of his trousers.

A new myriad of scents danced past her nose — saddle leather, smoke, and pine needles mixed with sheer maleness. It was such an overpowering combination that she swayed slightly in the saddle.

"We'd best get going." Jesse Hawling's baritone rumbled so close to Iris's ear that his breath stirred against her lobe. "There's no telling how soon the stagecoach driver will report your kidnapping and send the law after us."

Her lips parted in a gasp of astonishment. "I thought you *were* the law," she protested, twisting uncertainly in the saddle to meet his gaze. As his dark eyes raked over her, she experienced a whole new brand of weakness that had nothing to do with how many days she'd spent traveling and how little she'd eaten during that time.

"I am," he returned cheerfully, as he reached around her to lift his horse's reins, "but I'm off duty today, which is why you'll be owing me for my services." He urged his horse into a trot. His brothers did likewise, both riding well ahead of them.

"I, ah..." A surge of irritation took the worst edge off the awareness radiating between them. "I thought I made it clear I have no money, at least not at my current disposal." Other than the handful of coins pressed warmly against her bosom, of course.

"There are other ways to repay me." His bland gaze left hers to scan the terrain on either side of them. She could sense the watchfulness in him and wondered if there was a reason to be worried about their safety.

When the lull in their conversation started to feel awkward, she spoke up hesitantly. "Perhaps I could work off what I owe you." Surely, there was some sort of clerical work they could assign her at the sheriff's office where he was employed.

"Or you could marry me," he countered bluntly.

"M-marry you?" she stammered, wondering if she'd heard him correctly. She'd just come through a harrowing ordeal. Perhaps it had addled her ears. "I thought you understood that is *not* the real reason I summoned you."

He shrugged, as if the notion of becoming his bride was no big deal. "True. But once upon a time, you were pledged to another man by way of an arranged marriage. I reckon becoming a mail-order bride isn't a far cry from that."

But of course it was! She stared at him, aghast at the fact he couldn't see the difference. Her engagement to Edward Remington had been based on the comparable wealth, names, and social consequence of their families — all of which she highly doubted Jesse Hawling possessed. He was nothing more than a dusty cowboy with a shiny badge and a cocky attitude, and yet...

Good heavens! Only a fool could've missed the sheer male interest in his gaze as he surveyed her, and she was nobody's fool. This mountain man, with his faded shirt and scuffed boots, genuinely wanted to marry her. *Her*. It was a novel feeling, indeed, to be discussing the prospect of marriage with a man who desired the woman he was looking at. Edward

Remington, despite all his money and social consequence, had never shown a lick of personal interest in her.

"I hardly know what to say." Iris stared at him, utterly perplexed, knowing a woman of her background should not even entertain the notion of accepting such a preposterous offer for her hand. From the looks of him, he'd likely not bring more to their union than the horse they were sitting on.

He removed his hat and inclined his head at her. "Since I happen to be in the market for a wife, I'd be much obliged if you'd say yes." Though his words were humble, his gaze held a mocking twinkle. "As a deputy, I also happen to be in the position to help you fight back against your bloody uncle." He clapped his hat back on his head, a cocky grin twisting the edges of his hard mouth.

She caught her lower lip between her teeth, wanting to believe the last part of what he'd said. Oh, how she wanted to believe that the good Lord had heard her prayers and sent her a champion at long last! She'd just not imagined he could come in the form of such a humble cowboy. Or a husband.

He rounded a bend with his horse, forcing her to squint against the sunlight as she met his gaze again. "Do you truly wish to marry me, Jesse Hawling?" Logic told her there was the distinct possibility that he was just having his fun with her. Not too long ago, she'd brushed aside his attempt at gallantry as if he was nothing more than a fly. Surely he'd not forgotten her poor treatment of him. Was this his way of getting back at her?

His gaze dropped to the lower lip she was still nibbling with worry. "I do. Why do you act so surprised?"

"Well, for one thing, I'm not accustomed to running across men your age who are overly anxious to settle down." Was he even as old as her one and twenty years?

"I am two and twenty, ma'am, and more than ready to take on the burden of a wife."

"The burden?" she choked, still unsure if he was being serious or not. It was difficult to read his expression with the way his Stetson was riding so low on his forehead, keeping his eyes mostly in the shadow of his hat brim.

"Indeed." His answer was swift and matter-of-fact. "I have it on good account that all women are nothing but trouble."

The way his mouth twitched as he spoke made her realize he was, indeed, having fun at her expense. "You're a horrible man," she declared softly, feeling the sudden urge to laugh along with him.

"The worst of the worst," he agreed silkily. "Which is why you're going to agree to marry me."

"Why?" She shook her head at him, wanting desperately to understand. "We barely know each other, and I fear you were painfully on point about the trouble I will bring you."

He arched a challenging brow at her. "The truth isn't near as nice as pretending to be your knight in shining armor, so how about we let it go at that?"

She glanced away. "Actually, I'd rather have the truth, please. I'm done pretending." Way too much of her life had been about posturing and putting on airs. For once, she wanted to know where she truly stood.

"Very well." Jesse bent his head closer to speak cheek-to-cheek with her. "I'm not merely in the market for a wife. I'm gunning to hitch myself to a wealthy one."

Ouch! Her heart sank, making her wish she hadn't been so anxious to hear the truth, after all. "It is possible my fortune is gone forever, Deputy." She spoke in a cool, clipped tone. Since they'd agreed to speak the truth to each other, he might as well hear one of her harshest truths.

"Understood." For a man who'd so baldly shared his aspirations to marry for wealth, he sounded singularly unperturbed about her revelation. "Which brings me to my other reason for wanting to marry you. It's a far worse reason than the first, so I will again offer to spare your feelings by keeping it to myself."

"Oh?" Visions of being carnally mauled by him made her blush. Hard. "Well, don't hold back now." Her voice was dry. "You might as well share every sordid detail of what you intend to do with me."

"Well, here it is, Miss Hildebrand. I despise the way Edward Remington treated you. So much that I'd like nothing more than to rub his blasted nose in everything he gave up when he walked away from you. And I can't think of a better way of doing that, than to marry you myself and parade your lovely self in front of him every chance I get."

It wasn't exactly a declaration of affection, but it was certainly a more impassioned reason for marrying her than the mere chance of recovering her lost fortune someday. His anger with Edward also went a long way towards soothing her bruised heart.

She found herself swaying toward the glint in his wickedly daring gaze. "Although I never once imagined myself marrying for vengeance, the vain and petty side of me wants to say yes," she confessed.

"Then we have a deal, Miss Hildebrand?" He held out a hand, as if preparing to shake on a business arrangement.

"Isn't this a little sudden?" she inquired breathlessly. Her heart fluttered as she stared at his tanned, capable looking fingers.

"Yes, but acting swiftly is our best hope of fighting back against your uncle," he returned evenly. "Marrying me will give me a legal claim to your fortune. That is, if you truly wish for me to pick up that particular sword and start swinging on your behalf."

For a man who only minutes earlier claimed to be marrying her for her money, he sure possessed a chivalrous streak. She reached for his hand and lightly clasped it instead of shaking it. "What I want more than anything else right now, Deputy, is a bath." She gave him a rueful smile. They'd agreed to speak the truth to each other. That was the truth.

"I reckon that's something even a poor man can arrange for his bride-to-be." He treated her to such a lazy, indulgent smile that her heart thumped erratically in response. His fingers tightened around hers. "I assume this also means we've come to an understanding on the matter of marriage, Miss Hildebrand?"

"I believe we have. It seems like a fair enough trade," she teased. "My desire for a bath in exchange for your hope of becoming a wealthy man someday." Despite her attempt to keep the air light between them, her voice ended on a decidedly bitter note.

"Would you have preferred that I lied about my intentions toward you?" he inquired somberly.

"No." She turned her face away from him to stare blindly across the foothills they were traversing. "Never. I've had enough falsehoods and subterfuge to last me a lifetime. From now on, I prefer the truth, even when it hurts." Which it did. In that moment, Iris would have given anything to have Jesse Hawling declare his undying devotion to her. However, their forthcoming marriage was not one made in Heaven. They each had something the other wanted. She needed his protection; he wanted her wealth. That was all there was to it. Nothing more. Nothing less. She'd be wise to remember it in the coming days.

"Fine. Then allow me to say this." He bent his head beside hers once again. "Until yesterday, I was in the market for a wealthy wife. After I received your telegram, however, I was only in the market for one wealthy woman in particular. You."

"Why? As I've said before, my fortune might very well be gone forever." A new thought struck Iris, making her shiver. "What then? Will you seek to have our union annulled?"

"No." It was a single syllable, but he uttered it without hesitation. "My word is good. Once I give it, I'll never go back on it."

"Even if it means being saddled to a penniless woman until the end of your days?"

"Even then." Again, he spoke without hesitation.

"You're a very confusing man," she sighed.

"As well as hard-headed, short-tempered, irritating, and everything in between, or so I've been told on a number of occasions." Though she wasn't looking at him, he sounded as if he was grinning again. "What you see is what you get, princess. So if that bothers you too much between here and the altar, you're more than welcome to change your mind."

Her last set of reservations evaporated at his humble reminder that he had no intention of forcing her hand. The rest of her strength followed. She found herself sagging against his shoulder. "Pray forgive me," she whispered. "It's been a very long journey."

Instead of answering, he tightened the arm he had hooked around her waist and drew her closer. "We have a little ways to go yet. You might as well rest."

❈

SHE AWOKE, SHIVERING, TO THE SCENT OF SMOKE.

Jesse Hawling was lightly jostling her shoulder. "We've made it to the mail-order bride agency, Miss Hildebrand. It's time to sign our marriage contract, if you're still willing."

She gave another violent shiver, wondering why it suddenly felt twenty degrees colder than it had earlier.

He quickly shrugged out of his leather vest and draped it around her shoulders. "It's not much," he confessed wryly, "but it's better than nothing."

She accepted the vest gratefully and drew it more snugly

around her. It was a kind gesture coming from a man who didn't possess much. What little he had, though, he seemed willing to share.

"Where are your brothers, and why is it so cold?" This time, her teeth chattered when she spoke.

"They went back to work at the inn, and it's cold because we're high in the Christmas Mountains. It's always colder up here than in the valley." He swung himself from his horse and reached for her as soon as his boots hit the ground. "Come. It'll be warmer inside."

He led her through the front door of a plain adobe storefront. They were met on the other side by a tall, spindly man with silver hair. He took one look at her and whistled.

"Jesse Hawling, you dirty dog! You never mentioned how lovely your intended is."

He shrugged off-handedly. "The topic didn't come up."

Still looking amazed, the man beckoned them toward a rickety desk in the center of the room, glancing often in her direction. "I'm Clink Redwood, ma'am, the owner of this agency. All I need for you to do is sign each line on this contract that I've marked with an X." His expression turned sly. "Then you'll need to pay up, Jesse."

Trying not to appear as if she was staring, Iris watched out of the corner of her eye as her groom-to-be removed a wad of money from the pocket of his denim trousers and proceeded to peel off several bills. For a poor man, it was an awfully large roll. What had he done to acquire it? Rob a bank?

"I'll be needing a receipt for that amount," he informed the matchmaker tersely.

"Coming right up, Deputy." Mr. Redwood produced another sheet of paper and uncapped his inkwell.

"And the name of the nearest dressmaker, if it wouldn't be too much trouble. My new wife will undoubtably have need of a few garments."

"Certainly." The older gentleman rattled off a name and address that sounded as humble and countrified as their surroundings. Iris instinctively knew the dressmaker wouldn't be tailoring anything as fine as the dress she was already wearing.

"One more thing," Jesse inquired smoothly. "Is there any truth to the rumor that Old Man Crocker on the other side of the mountain is knocking at death's door?"

"Far as anyone can tell." Mr Redwood reached up to run a hand through his silver hair, setting it on end. "It's a dead shame, too, since he has no family to look after him in his final hours."

"Figured that. Maybe my wife and I will pay him a visit soon."

Iris had no idea why her husband-to-be was so anxious to introduce her to a stranger on his death bed, but there was no opportunity to ask. Mr. Redwood hustled them through the rest of their paperwork. Then he accompanied them on an old, reddish-brown mare to an adobe church that wasn't much bigger than the bedchamber Iris had grown up in.

Jesse gave the matchmaker an abrupt nod. "You go on inside ahead of us. We'll join you shortly."

"Aye, aye, Deputy." Mr. Redwood delivered a mock salute, tethered his horse, and jogged up the church stairs two at a time.

Iris watched Jesse in puzzled silence. Apparently, he wanted to speak to her alone before their wedding ceremony, but why?

"I have a confession to make," Jesse announced quietly. They remained seated on his horse, their faces only inches away from each other. However, he suddenly seemed to be having a difficult time meeting her eye.

"What is it?" Iris whispered. Her heart trembled at the seriousness of his expression.

"The biggest reason I felt compelled to answer your call for help was because of an inquiry I sent to a sheriff in New York on your behalf. He's the one who notified me you were being shipped to an asylum, and there was just no way I could stand by and let that happen."

"Why?" It was the same question she'd been asking again and again for the past few hours. "I mean, for all you knew, my confinement was justified."

"Two reasons." He met her gaze squarely. "There was nothing wrong with your mental faculties the day we met; and not too long ago, I was mistakenly confined to the asylum myself."

"You?" she gasped. *Why?*

He briefly recounted a mind-boggling tale of how he'd innocently ingested a hallucinatory herb that had caused his family to doubt his sanity. "So there you have it," he concluded. "The ugly truth. Every last detail of it. If you follow me into the church, you'll be marrying a man who was once confined to the very asylum you narrowly avoided. If that fact gives you any doubt—"

"It doesn't," she interrupted, feeling her eyes grow damp. Quite the opposite. It gave her a beautiful sense of peace to know that the good Lord had indeed heard and answered her prayers. The cocky cowboy sitting astride the horse behind her was no storybook hero, but he'd most definitely been sent to her rescue. Her last doubts about him vanished. "If anything, your story strengthens my resolve to marry you."

He arched a brow at her. "Do tell."

She had no idea if he was a man of faith, so she wasn't sure he would understand. "Do you believe things happen for a reason?"

He shrugged. "Sometimes, I reckon."

"What if the reason you suffered at the asylum the way you did was to prepare you for coming to my rescue?"

"Well, that's one way of looking at it." He studied her in bemusement. "Does this mean we're still getting married?"

She nodded shyly.

"I reckon we better get moving, then." He leaped to the ground, then reached up to assist her down. "They're probably wondering what's taking us so long."

She took the arm he offered and allowed him to lead her inside the church. A man dressed in a plain brown suit met them at the altar and led them in the age-old ceremony. He reverently recited a few scriptures and officiated their exchange of wedding vows.

"I now pronounce you man and wife. You may kiss your bride, Deputy Hawling."

Ignoring Iris's sharp intake of breath, Jesse swooped in to brush his hard mouth against hers. "Now you are mine." His voice was low and husky with satisfaction.

His. She drew a tremulous breath, hardly knowing what to make of her new role. The minister produced a marriage certificate for them to sign and accompanied it with a fervent promise to keep their union hush-hush as long as possible. Though there was no way he knew Iris's whole story, apparently Clink Redwood had impressed upon him that her safety depended on his discretion.

To her further gratitude, her new husband borrowed a choir robe, of all things, to shield her against the cold as he rode away from the church with her. She didn't want to think about how ridiculous she looked; she was just grateful for the additional barrier against the breeze.

To her surprise, they set their course for the creature Jesse kept referring to as Old Man Crocker. What an odd name! They were soon riding up a sandy driveway to a modest-sized ranch home in desperate need of repairs. The paint was peeling, and the porch roof looked like it might fall in at any moment. However, the rickety stairs held firm when she and her new husband ascended them to reach the front door.

No one answered when they knocked. After a few tries, Jesse twisted the doorknob and discovered it was unlocked. "What's he thinking?" he muttered. "Out here alone without so much as a locked door between him and any rogue that might bumble through!"

Her new husband nudged her behind him as he pushed open the door and called out, "Mr. Crocker? Are you home?"

They made their way into a musty smelling living room crowded with outdated odds and ends of furniture. The bookshelves were, by far, the most interesting feature. They were literally crammed with volumes, albeit dusty and cobweb-drenched ones. Iris's fingers itched to explore their titles.

There was one additional interesting feature to the room — Mr. Crocker, himself. He spun his chair around to face them as they entered, making an ominous creaking sound. Then he lifted the rifle in his arms to level it at them. The papery skin at the edges of his eyes was creased with annoyance.

"I didn't call for a deputy," he snarled.

"I'm not here as a deputy, sir. This is a social call."

"Like I believe that!" The older gentleman gave a loud *harrumph*. "If you came to whack me over the head in the hopes of jumping a claim on the place like the last scallawag, then you've made a terrible error in judgment." His long, gray beard quivered with righteous indignation as he spoke. "Because I don't plan on going down without a fight."

"Nope. Didn't come for that reason." Though Iris was trembling from head to toe, Jesse Hawling didn't look overly concerned about staring down the barrel of a gun. "Word around town is that you're at death's door, so we thought we'd come pay you a visit. That's all."

"We're all at death's door," the old farmer muttered, "from the moment we come squalling into this miserable world."

"We also heard you don't have any family to look after you, so my new bride and I are here to offer our assistance." Iris couldn't have been more astonished. His words were news to her. "We were married just this evening and don't yet have a home to call our own. So we'll gladly prepare your meals, keep the house clean, and make some much-needed repairs in exchange for room and board, if you're willing."

Mr. Crocker slowly lowered his rifle. "Well, that's an offer no one else has come by here to make."

Jesse's mouth quirked. "If you happen to own a bathtub, you'll additionally earn my wife's undying gratitude. She traveled all the way from New York to get here, and I have it on good account that she'll give anything short of her soul to be clean again."

Mr. Crocker gave a delighted cackle. "I like you." He laid his weapon sideways across his knees. "I like you enough to say yes to your outlandish proposal and give it a test run. Mind you," he warned, "if you pull anything foolish, I won't think twice about plugging a hole in you and burying your carcass some place they'll never find you."

"I'd probably do the same, if I was in your shoes," Jesse returned mildly.

"Not certain who started that rumor about me being at death's door," the older man continued irritably. "I may not be getting any younger, but I'm still kicking."

"I can see that." Jesse held out a hand. "In all truth, it'll also be a good while before my wife and I are in the position to afford a house of our own." He grimaced. "Meaning you'll be stuck with us as long as you like. That said, I can be a pretty useful fellow to have around, if I say so myself."

Mr. Crocker gave a short, jerky nod. "How about you start by filling the firewood bin out front? When you're finished, the tub is in the kitchen, and my spare room is down the hall." He waved a knobby hand in the general direction of the hallway.

Spare room? As in one and only one? Iris caught her breath at the realization that the aging farmer expected her and Jesse to share the same room. Which she supposed made sense, since they were married now...

The most mind boggling thing of all, though, was the fact that her new husband had somehow talked his way into a roof over their heads, one they wouldn't be required to share with her former affianced. Right up to this very moment, she assumed they would be staying at the Christmas Mountain Inn, where he'd resided during her first visit to Texas.

"Alright, then." Jesse angled his head at the front door, giving Iris one of his crooked grins she was quickly growing to adore. "I'll be seeing to the firewood next."

Hurrying after him, Iris stepped outside into the cool mountain breeze. "Well, Deputy Hawling, I will admit to being impressed." *With you.* She rested her elbows on the porch railing and watched him pick up a discarded ax on the front lawn.

He shot her a puzzled look before swinging the ax in a large arc and bringing it down on an enormous log. The piece of wood split into two pieces that toppled to their sides on the ground. "You're welcome to start calling me Jesse, now that we're married and all."

"Why, certainly, Jesse, if that is what you prefer."

"It is, Iris." His dark gaze caressed her as he repositioned the smaller pieces of wood and brought the ax down a second time. "Now about whatever it is that has you so impressed." He winked at her. "By all means, sing my praises as loudly as you wish."

She chuckled. "I was just going to say that it's quite a feat, talking your way into both a marriage and a home — all in the same afternoon. I've never met a man quite like you."

"Of course you haven't," he teased, swinging the ax again. "I'm one-of-a-kind, darlin'."

She caught her breath at the easy way the endearment rolled from his mouth. Though the mountain breeze continued to blow, she found herself warming in steady degrees at the sight of her brawny groom putting his back into his labor. He'd left his hat tossed on a rocker on the porch, and his sleeves were rolled up, revealing nicely chiseled arms.

One-of-a-kind, indeed. Her heart sang at the knowledge that she'd happened upon someone very special in Deputy Jesse Hawling. She'd wed a man who was cocky, stubborn, hard-working, and honest to a fault. She truly could've done worse — a whole lot worse — and almost had. Despite her new groom's lack of wealth, she had a niggling sensation that her father would've approved of their union.

For the first time in many months, she tasted hope.

CHAPTER 4: COUNTRY LIFE
JESSE

Though it was May, it was still cool on the mountain in the evenings, so Jesse didn't think twice about building a fire on the hearth in the kitchen. The crackling fire made it easy to heat several buckets of water at the same time to draw a bath for his new bride.

As he gazed curiously at his surroundings, it dawned on him that he was standing inside a very well constructed room. Someone had gone to a great deal of effort carving a motif of elk, rabbits, and pine trees around the edges of the cabinet drawers and doors. Because of his oldest brother's vocation as a furniture maker, Jesse understood how much time and elbow grease had gone into the project. He'd watched Jonah whittle for hours on end just to complete a single drawer cover.

Though the room was in desperate need of a good dusting and mopping, it was well laid out. Besides the wide hearth and fat cook stove, it boasted a spacious preparation counter in the center of the room, a large washing area, and a corner pantry. After all that, there was still room left over for a round trestle table pushed against the far wall with a trio of stools resting beneath it. The room's finest feature, however, was the wall of windows overlooking Old Man Crocker's rim property. One of the windows was located directly over the kitchen sink, making it possible for a person to gaze across the canyon walls to the valley below while working. Or in Jesse's case, he could venture an occasional peek outside to check on his wife, who was busy picking wildflowers.

For a high-society debutante, she seemed to be acclimating rather quickly to country life. He watched as she bent to pluck another stem from the ground, which she added to the others in her hand. Then she buried her face in the blooms and breathed deeply. It was such an artless little gesture that he was thoroughly enchanted.

Old Man Crocker puttered in and out of the room several times, eyeing Jesse's stance at the window in contemplative silence. On his second trip, he delivered a stack of towels and washcloths. They were faded different shades of dingy brown and gray, with several loose threads hanging from their corners. However, they were clean.

After a pause, Mr. Crocker dragged one of the stools over to set it beside the tub of water Jesse was preparing. Then he plopped the stack of towels on it and left the room as silently as he'd entered it. He reappeared a few minutes later to drape a frock of faded blue cotton over the towels.

This time, he paused on his way back out the door to wave a gnarled finger at Jesse. "It ain't nothin' fancy, but that wife of yours is gonna need somethin' to wear while her other things dry."

"Right." Jesse grimaced at the reminder that they'd arrived at the Crocker homestead with nothing but the clothes on their backs. "I should probably ride back into town to collect a few supplies from my apartment over the jailhouse."

"Or you can jes' borrow a few of my old things and worry about that on the morrow." Old Man Crocker gave one of his dry cackles. "Just fer the record, I didn't buy yer yarn about payin' me a visit. Not for a blessed second. No one gives a rat's hind end about a perfect stranger. So whenever you're ready to fess up about why you really rode all the way out here, I'm all ears."

Jesse shrugged and pivoted away from the window. "It's true that I came to check on you, but it was mostly to find out how accurate the rumors were about you not having any heirs. I was hoping to be the first man to jump a claim on the place after you passed."

The aging farmer gave Jesse a sharp look. "After I passed, eh? You weren't lookin' to speed me on to Glory, then?"

"Absolutely not!" Jesse stared at him in amazement. "Exactly how many fellas have tried to harass you into an early grave?"

Old Man Crocker gave a gusty sigh and rubbed a hand across his shaggy beard. "Too many to keep track of. I'd say a good two or three per month, at least."

Jesse scowled as he removed another bucket of water from the fire. "I really wish you'd tipped off the law about this sooner, Mr. Crocker." He pitched the scalding water into the galvanized steel tub and bent to test the water with two fingers. If it was his bath, he'd have jumped right in. But since it was for his bride, he decided it could use a few more buckets of warm water to bring it to the perfect temperature.

"I jes' finished tellin' ya." The elderly man gave a toothy grin. "I expect things will git better, now that I got my own deputy livin' on the premises."

"They will," Jesse promised. His heart warmed at the pride in the old fella's voice. It was a novel emotion to actually feel needed. He'd spent much of his life serving as the pesky younger brother, whose tagalong presence his brothers had merely tolerated. Then there'd been his stint in the asylum last year, when both his father and brothers had assumed he'd gone mad. Helping out Old Man Crocker was the first time in a long time that Jesse didn't feel any pressure to be anything he wasn't. Way up here in the mountains, he had nothing to prove and no one to impress, other than his lovely new bride, of course.

"Good. It's settled then." Mr. Crocker dusted his hands in satisfaction. "Allow me to show my appreciation for your deputy oversight by making do with what we got on hand for the evening. I got plenty of supplies for us all."

Jesse gave him a sheepish look. "That's mighty kind of you, Mr. Crocker, but I should probably go fetch a travel bag, at least. We really don't want to be a burden—"

"You're not," his host interrupted. "I know you're poor and proud, Deputy, but it won't kill you to accept my hospitality for one bloody evening. I'll be back with a bar of soap in a bit."

Jesse stared after him in amazement. Then, shaking his head, he returned to pouring the final few buckets of water into his wife's bath. Sure enough, Old Man Crocker returned with the thickest bar of freshly cut lye soap Jesse had ever seen. He wondered if the widower had made it himself.

"I reckon it's time for me to fetch Mrs. Hawling for her bath." Jesse surveyed the tub and bathing supplies in satisfaction. It wasn't the style in which his lovely wife was accustomed to living, but it would satisfy her basic needs.

Old Man Crocker nodded, looking as pleased as Jesse felt. "I'll go gather the eggs my hens laid this afternoon."

Jesse glanced up in surprise. "May I help with that, sir?"

"Nah. You'd best stay close, in case your purty wife needs anything. Iffin you or she want to wash your clothes, my washboard and bucket are in the bottom of the pantry."

Good idea. Fortunately, the kitchen was plumbed for running cold well water, so it took no time for Jesse to fill the laundry bucket and carry it out to the back porch. Since his new bride's travel bags had been left on the stagecoach, he'd best launder her unmentionables while she bathed. Come morning, he'd hightail it into town and see about getting a change of clothing sewn up for her. Fortunately, he'd scrimped and saved nearly every penny he'd ever earned, so he could well afford to outfit his new wife.

He met her skipping up the porch stairs as he was heading out the front door.

"Look what I found!" She brandished her fistful of wildflowers beneath his nose. "Aren't they lovely?"

"Fetching," he agreed, drinking in the sight of her. There were grass stains on her fingertips and a healthy flush to her cheeks. The mountain breeze had wreaked havoc on her hair. Loose tendrils were flying in all directions. She was the loveliest, most disheveled creature he'd ever laid eyes on.

She brushed past him, making him long to reach for her hand to slow her promenade across the rickety porch. However, he resisted the temptation.

"Do you suppose Mr. Crocker owns a vase?"

"I reckon we can stick 'em in a glass if he doesn't." Jesse held out his hands for the blooms. "Here. Let me worry about the flowers while you freshen up. I drew you a bath."

"Gladly." Their fingers brushed as she transferred the bouquet to him, making the air between them radiate with new awareness. "I really like it here, Jesse." She drenched him with a happy smile. "I hope we don't have to leave anytime soon."

He held open the front door for her. "It's only a little country farm, Iris. A far cry from what you're used to, I'm afraid."

"It's perfect," she said so quickly that he scanned her features in concern.

"No, Iris. It's not." He dropped a hand to her arm, making her pause. "I dare say this old place has very few of the comforts you're accustomed to." The novelty would soon wear off, reality would set in, and then what?

She tipped her face up to his. "I hear what you're saying, but this old place happens to have a few features I've always dreamed of, too, Jesse. Things that money can't buy."

I seriously doubt that. He raised his brows at her. "Such as?"

"The walls are finally down," she returned evenly. "I can see all the way to the horizon without having to look through the slats of a fence or the iron bars of a gate. For the first time in my life, I'm not at the risk of being snatched and held for ransom. I'm truly free." With that, she ducked away from his grasp and sailed into the house.

He stared after her with his mouth agape. It took him a moment to collect his wits enough to follow her. "Mr. Crocker unearthed an old dress for you. I'm not certain it'll even fit, but—"

"Oh!" she squealed the moment they reached the kitchen. She hurried forward to snatch up the cotton gown, holding it high in the air. "It's a vintage dress. A life-sized version of the one I used to dress my favorite doll in back home. Is it truly meant for me to wear?"

Jesse was vastly amused by her show of girlish delight in such a plain garment. It was utterly captivating the way she continued to treat everything new she experienced like it was part of some grand adventure. All he could do was hope her natural well of excitement wouldn't wear off too soon.

"According to our host, yes. You may wear the dress with his blessing."

By the time Old Man Crocker returned to the house with his basket of eggs, both Iris and Jesse were bathed and dressed. She remained sitting by the fire with her hair draped in damp ringlets around her shoulders, so it could dry; while Jesse emptied the tub and wiped the dampness from the floor from their bath.

"You look so much like her, it's uncanny." Mr. Crocker stood riveted in the doorway to the kitchen, looking transfixed.

Iris stood and treated him to a perfect curtsey. "Like who, sir?"

"My Phyllis, may she rest in peace." He made the sign of the cross over his heart and finished stepping into the room.

"Oh, Mr. Crocker!" Iris gave a wistful sigh. "I had no idea you'd lent something so precious to me."

"It's quite alright," he assured, shuffling farther into the room. "It does my heart good to see it gettin' some use again. No point in it fadin' away in the storage trunk or waitin' fer the moths to carry it off piece by piece." He deposited his basket of eggs on the kitchen cabinet. "I reckon we should stir something up for dinner. What tickles your fancy, Mrs. Hawling?"

She jolted at his use of her married name, but she quickly recovered. "Well, our last cook was a French lady who stirred up the most divine *Coq Au Vin*. I declare it was second only to her *Cassoulet* with duck sausage. For dessert, more often than not, she would whip up a fresh *Pear Tarte Tatin* that she..." Her voice dwindled as she noted how wide their host's jaws were gaping.

It took him a moment to collect his wits and snap his mouth closed. "Have you ever cooked anything, Mrs. Hawling?"

"Well, no," she answered slowly, her smile slipping. "I wasn't allowed, but how hard can it be?"

"What exactly were you allowed to do, yer royal highness?" he teased. "Besides pickin' flowers and curtseyin' and such?"

"Now you're just having fun at my expense." She waved a hand and sighed. "I can sing, play the pianoforte, speak in all the romance languages, paint watercolors, and dance.

Anything else you need me to do, you'll have to show me. But never fear. I'm a quick study."

Grinning from ear-to-ear, Mr. Crocker angled his head at his basket of eggs. "Wouldn't mind teaching you how to make a proper quiche for dinner, but it's gonna cost you."

"I, er, have a few coins to my name, sir." She glanced toward the garments she'd discarded on the chair earlier and scowled when she found them missing. "Jesse?" She turned her startled gaze to him. "Where is my gown?"

"Airing out on the back porch."

"And my other things?"

"I washed them and hung them out to dry, as well."

Her squeak of mortification caught him by surprise. "You laundered my unmentionables?"

He dug out the handful of money she'd left piled beneath her neatly folded garments. "Perhaps these are what you're looking for, madam?" He strode across the room to drop them into her hand.

Nodding and flushing prettily, she spun back to Old Man Crocker with a pair of coins pinched between her thumb and forefinger.

However, he shook his head vehemently. "By cost, I was referring to yer music, ma'am. Was of a mind to have you sing for yer dinner."

"Oh!" She caught her breath and hastily returned the handful of coins to Jesse, to his immense surprise. "In that case..."

While he debated what to do with the money that his new bride had so carelessly tossed at him, she hummed a few notes and launched into an old church hymn.

Swaying back and forth in time to the music, Old Man Crocker started to crack eggs and dump them into a mixing bowl. He motioned for Iris to join him. Looking delighted, she reached for her first egg and cracked it against the side of the bowl. Alas, she didn't move quickly enough, and the yolk gave a squishy splat as it landed on the cabinet.

"I'm so sorry," she murmured, pausing her singing and looking stricken.

"Again!" Mr. Crocker instructed firmly, handing her another egg.

With a nervous chuckle, she cracked her second egg. This time it made it into the bowl. "I did it!" She waved her hands in the air in triumph and reached for another egg.

"Looks like you're a natural." Mr. Crocker winked at her as they continued to sing and crack eggs together.

Jesse watched the show, enjoying himself more than he had at the one traveling circus he'd attended.

"A natural at what?" his new bride moaned, turning his way to wiggle her sticky fingers in the air at him. "Making messes?"

"Who isn't?" Mr. Crocker retorted airily. "As my wife always liked to say, a messy kitchen is the sign of a cook who cooks."

They ended up producing a quiche brimming with ham and cheese that was both light and delicious.

"Thank you, Mr. Crocker!" After the three of them finished dining at the small trestle table against the kitchen wall, Iris rose to give her instructor a quick hug. "I don't believe I've ever enjoyed a lesson more."

He reddened and patted the hand she'd left resting on his shoulder.

As the evening progressed, Jesse's longing grew to have his new bride alone. Once the two of them retired to their bedchamber, however, her smiles and chatter disappeared. He figured it had something to do with the oversized four-poster bed in the center of the room.

"Never fear, Mrs. Hawling. I plan to sleep on the floor."

He parked his tired limbs on a bench at the foot of the bed to remove his boots.

"You most certainly will not!" She looked aghast at the notion. "You'll catch your death of cold down there, and heaven only knows what else might come creeping and crawling its way through the dark."

He was both pleased and tickled by her wifely concerns, but more puzzled than ever as to where she expected him to sleep. "Are you ready to be completely mine, then?" When all else failed, he tended to fall back on blunt speaking.

She blushed a deep crimson. "All I'm saying is that you don't belong on the floor, Deputy Hawling. It's a big bed." She studied it critically, still blushing. "Maybe we can toss a pillow between us or..."

"Don't mind if we do," he assured quietly. He was disappointed by her response, of course, but he liked the idea of being that much closer to his lovely bride.

Sleeping in such proximity to her, however, did not ward off their first disagreement the next morning. If anything, a night of being so close to her, yet so far away, left him cranky and on edge.

"You wish to purchase me a new gown?" She eyed his threadbare clothing in dismay. "What about your own clothing, Jesse? You are in far worse need of a new outfit than me!"

"So?" He jutted his chin, wondering what in tarnation he'd said to put such a defensive note in her voice. Weren't women supposed to enjoy gifts? "I want you to have a new gown."

She slapped her hands down on her too-thin hips. "Not on your life! I'll not be allowing you to spend your last dime on me, while you continue to do without." When he didn't immediately answer, she demanded, "When was the last time you bought a new shirt for yourself?"

"What I choose to live with or without is my business," he growled.

"It was," she corrected, tossing her head, "until you married me. Now it's my business, too."

"But you're accustomed to nice things," he protested. "I'm not." *Just let me buy you the blasted dress and be done with it!*

Her eyes bugged out. "Be that as it may, I wouldn't feel right accepting such a gift, if you're not willing to at least replace your coat and boots. You made it very clear to me from the beginning that money was tight. I can live with that. What I can't live with is one of us doing all the taking and none of the giving."

Her sense of fairness caught him off guard. "Well, then," he muttered in amazement. "I reckon I could spare the coin for a new coat and a pair of boots, if you insist."

"I do. Thank you, Jesse." She smiled so sweetly at him that he stepped closer to brush his mouth against hers.

And found he couldn't immediately bring himself to step away. She was so soft, warm, and caring — not at all the hard-hearted termagant he'd originally pegged her for.

"What are you doing to me, Iris?" He spoke against her lips, reveling in her nearness and flowery scent.

"This," she whispered. Twining her arms around his neck, she pressed her lips ever-so-gently to his once again.

With a low groan of surrender, he took what she offered. It was a long time before they made it into town to visit the tailor.

CHAPTER 5: COMMON ENEMIES

IRIS

Iris was well aware that her ladylike accomplishments didn't exactly get the cows fed or meals put on the table. However, she worked like crazy over the next several weeks to make herself more useful. Half of the time, she felt like she was just tagging along while the men did most of the work. They did eventually turn over a few of the smaller tasks to her, like the egg gathering, which she adored.

The speckled hens and brightly plumed banty roosters were very entertaining to watch. She named them all and even coaxed a few of them into letting her pet their sleek, feathered necks and backs.

One afternoon, as she was putting the last egg into her basket, she jolted in surprise to find Jesse leaning on the fence with one boot propped on the lowest rung. The song she'd been singing died on her lips as she watched him move the piece of straw in his mouth from one side to the other.

"When did you get home?" she demanded, trying to tamp down on the ridiculous surge of joy in her chest. He'd been putting in longer hours than usual at the station, due to an ongoing horse rustling case.

"Few minutes ago." He beckoned her closer to give her a quick peck on the lips. "Why? Did you miss me, Mrs. Hawling?"

"I might have." She unconsciously hummed a few more bars of her song.

"So you really do sing to the chickens, eh?" he teased. "I've heard rumors."

"They enjoy it," she announced with a lofty toss of her head.

"Is that so?" His grin widened.

"Indeed, they do, Mr. Hawling. Just ask Mr. Crocker. He'll confirm that our egg supply has significantly increased since my arrival here."

He arched a brow at her. "So you're saying...?"

"Happy chickens lay more eggs." She smoothed a hand over the fabric of his shirt. "It's a good thing, too, because a certain deputy sure knows how to put them away."

He caught her hand and pressed it to his heart. "It's also rumored that you've named all seven of Mr. Crocker's cows and have been enjoying some fairly lengthy conversations with his horses."

She gave her husband a secretive smile, setting her basket of eggs down on the ground. "I can neither confirm nor deny those claims, and good luck getting a confession out of the animals."

He chuckled and tossed aside his piece of straw, leaning in for another kiss. This one was tender and lingering. Afterward, he tipped back his head to gaze deeply into her eyes.

She adored the way the wind was whipping at his black hair, blowing one wave rakishly over his eyes. Unable to resist, she reached up to tuck it beneath the brim of his hat once again.

He palmed her cheek, running a thumb across the curve of her chin. "Just so you know, I never got around to paying a visit to that attorney today, like I said I would. Got too busy, I reckon." His voice was rueful. "I'll try to get to it tomorrow. Lord knows you deserve justice for all that's been done to you."

"I, ah..." Iris caught her lower lip between her teeth, longing to say what was on her heart but unsure of how he would take it. However, they'd promised to always be truthful with each other, so she plunged onward. "The truth is, I'm not in a terrible hurry to get started on our court case, Jesse. I hope you don't think I'm trying to go back on my word when I say that." She glanced away from his searching gaze, scrambling for a way to make him understand all that was on her heart. "I know you've always said you aim to become a wealthy man, and you have every right to lay claim to my family's fortune now that we're wed. It's just that..." *Oh, dear!* She found herself blinking back tears.

"Talk to me, Iris." Lightly pinching her chin, he steered her gaze back to his. "I thought we agreed to be honest with each other, even when it isn't easy."

"I don't want you to be angry with me," she murmured damply.

"I can handle a little anger, Mrs. Hawling, so go on and spill whatever it is you feel you gotta say."

"I like things how they are, Jesse!" The words burst from her like a flood. "I'm sorry if that's not what you want to hear me say, but it's true."

His dark gaze narrowed on hers. "You like living here," he stated carefully, "on a farm we don't even own."

She nodded fiercely. "I've never been happier."

"Gathering eggs and taking lukewarm baths in a tub in the kitchen?" he pressed, looking monumentally puzzled.

"Yes. I like it a lot. Does that make me crazy?"

"Please don't ever use that word around me again."

Good gracious! She hadn't intended to make any reference

to his asylum days. "I'm sorry, Jesse. It was a very poor choice of words—"

"And quit apologizing." He guided her face back to his so he could seal his mouth over hers. "I missed you today," he muttered between kisses. "I miss you every day I have to be gone. I count the minutes until I can return home to you."

Her heart soared at how ridiculously close he'd come to declaring his feelings for her. He cared, no matter how little he said on the topic. She was glad to hear the longing in his voice, since she'd been busy falling for him since the moment he'd rescued her from that dratted stagecoach.

"I missed you, too," she whispered. "So much."

"I reckon that settles it." Jesse raised his head, his dark eyes glowing with contentment. "If you truly don't mind us bunking here with Mr. Crocker and living on what I can provide with my deputy salary, then I see no reason to change a thing."

What he left unsaid took her breath away. Was he actually willing to give up his pursuit of her family fortune, just because she asked him to? It was a heady thought. It was also more proof of how much he'd come to care for her.

"That's exactly what I want, Jesse. Well, almost," she corrected softly.

He toyed with a strand of her hair. "What else do you want, Mrs. Hawling? By now, I think you realize I'd try to lasso the moon and stars, if you asked me to."

She hesitated to voice her next wish. Instead, she couched it in a question. "Have you ever dreamed of having a family someday, Jesse?" She paused a second before adding in a softer voice, "With me?"

He looked so stunned that she blushed. Wildly. For an answer, he leaped across the fence separating them to take her in his arms. "Only every hour of every day, Mrs. Hawling."

"Me, too," she whispered shyly. "I realize I don't know the

first thing about being a mother, any more than I know the first thing about tending animals and growing crops, but—"

"I'll show you, sweetheart." His arms tightened around her. "Not that I think you'll require much instruction. So far, you've done just fine figuring things out on your own. Very fine, indeed." He claimed her lips again, deepening their kiss as he finished unraveling her emotions.

TWO MONTHS LATER

Try as he might, Jesse couldn't hold off the inevitable forever. It was on a random Tuesday morning that he finally ran into Edward Remington on the street outside the post office.

"Good morning, Deputy." Edward jovially thrust out a hand. "How are you?"

"Never better." Jesse fought to keep his expression neutral, knowing it had been a good three months or longer since they'd last spoken. "How's Lacey and Malachi?" Come to think of it, he missed the little chap.

"Missing you and wondering what's been keeping you so busy that we never see you anymore." He cast a curious, sideways glance at Jesse as they fell into step with each other. "Tried asking your brothers what you've been up to lately, but they didn't seem to have anything of substance to add to the conversation." He shook his head. "Not that it's any of my business, but did you have some sort of falling out with Jack and Jonah?"

"What? No!" Jesse scowled. He and his brothers had been through thick and thin together. He seriously couldn't think of anything that could come between them, at least not permanently.

"Then why did you move out of the carriage house?"

Who said I moved out? Jesse shrugged. "As you well know, the sheriff and I have that loft apartment over the jailhouse."

"Which he swears you haven't used in months," Edward interjected.

"You've been checking up on me?" Jesse gaped at him. "Why does it matter to you where I live?"

"Because Lacey and I care about you," Edward exploded. "Call me a sentimental fool, but I consider you to be like family. Even little Malachi has been asking about his Uncle Jesse, wondering why you haven't paid him a visit in such a long while."

Shame burned through Jesse. Maybe he'd gone a little overboard on this whole avoidance thing. "If you insist on knowing, I've been staying across town with Old Man Crocker. There were some rogues coming around and acting all threatening, so I figured my presence would put an end to it. Plus, he had a lot of repairs and such that needed to be done to the place."

"You ol' soft-hearted kitten, you!" Edward gave a low whistle, looking suitably impressed. "But that still doesn't explain why you're avoiding us at the inn."

"I'm not avoiding you."

"It sure feels like it to Lacey and me." He snorted. "And Malachi."

"Way to rub it on thick," Jesse growled. "If you're trying to make me feel like the lowest cad on the planet, it's working."

"Good. I hope you feel bad enough about your ongoing absence to join us for dinner tonight."

Jesse hesitated so long that Edward waggled his finger in accusation. "Ha! I knew it. There's something else going on in your life, isn't there?"

"Yes. There's something else going on," he admitted reluctantly, "but I'm not at liberty to discuss it." *Yet.*

"Why not?"

"Because it involves the well-being of someone else besides me." The irony of the situation was not lost on Jesse. His mouth tightened at the recollection of the role Edward had played in putting Iris in such a precarious position.

"A woman, eh?"

"I didn't say that."

"You didn't have to. Most of the trouble men find themselves in has to do with some woman or another. Seriously, Jesse, if you need my help—"

"I don't," he assured so flatly that Edward's eyebrows shot heavenward.

"I mean it, Jesse. A loan, a favor, whatever you need. It's the least I can do to repay you for everything—"

"Just let it be. You've done enough already." It was impossible to keep the bitterness out of his tone, since Edward's refusal to marry Iris had endangered her very life. Not that Jesse would've preferred for her to end up married to anyone other than himself. *Argh! What a tangle!*

"Are we still talking about the trouble you're in?" Edward inquired quietly, "because it feels like we've moved on to another topic."

"I'm not in any trouble." Jesse had never been good at telling half-truths and he was fast growing weary of dancing around the root of the matter. "My wife, however, is." His jaw tightened. *Because of you.*

Edward abruptly halted their promenade. "You're married? Since when?"

"Since I felt like getting married."

"That's not a real answer." Edward gave a derisive snort. "I reckon you paid a visit to Clink's agency, eh? Because this town isn't exactly crawling with ladies."

"Yes, Clink assisted me."

"You sly dog, you. Sending off for a mail-order bride

without so much as a boo about it to the rest of us. I reckon all there's left for me to say on the topic is congratulations!"

"Thank you."

"Lacey is going to be furious, of course, once she hears we weren't invited to your wedding."

"We had our reasons for keeping it quiet."

"I figured that, since you already made it clear your wife is in some sort of trouble." Edward frowned thoughtfully. "Pray recall Lacey was in a heap of trouble, too, when she first stepped off the train with Malachi in her arms. You stood by us through it all, and we'll do the same for you. That's what family's for."

Jesse shook his head regretfully. "Although I appreciate the offer, I have a good reason for keeping you as far as possible from this particular situation. You're just going to have to take my word for it."

"Very well." Edward half turned away, then paused. "Will you at least bring your lovely new bride to dinner this evening, so we can meet her?"

"I'll think about it." Jesse blew out an irritated breath. He had to hand it to the fellow for being persistent.

"Good. We'll set two extra places at the table in the hopes that you'll be able to make it."

IRIS PALED SEVERAL SHADES WHEN JESSE RELAYED EDWARD'S invitation to dinner.

He hastened to add, "But this isn't New York, darlin'. We're under no obligation whatsoever to accept his invitation. You don't ever have to lay eyes on your former affianced again, if you don't want to."

"True, but I should go, anyway," she sighed. "From the

moment I arrived in town, it was inevitable that he and I would eventually have to face each other again."

"Perhaps, but that meeting does not, for any reason, have to take place this evening. Or tomorrow. Or the day after that."

She gave a breathy chuckle. "I'll confess, that's not what I was expecting you to say. Whatever happened to your desire for vengeance?" She specifically recalled him stating that he wanted to rub Edward's blasted nose in everything he'd lost when he'd refused to marry her.

"You happened, Iris. That's what." Jesse's jaw tightened. "And I have no plans to let you go. Ever."

It suddenly dawned on her that he was doing more than protecting her sensibilities. He clearly wasn't thrilled at the thought of having to witness her and Edward together in the same room again.

Hoping to reassure him, she teased, "So we'll face my dragons together."

Despite her attempt at keeping the conversation light, her heart was heavy as she changed into her best gown, the lavender silk with its cascading rows of lace. *I can do this.* Edward's rejection was a thing of the past. In some ways, she was grateful to him for ending their engagement. Otherwise, she might have never met and married Jesse.

To her enormous appreciation, Old Man Crocker insisted on lending them his wagon and a team of horses. It was so much better than riding side saddle all the way to the Christmas Mountain Inn, especially since both she and Jesse were wearing their finest outfits.

In addition to his new coat and boots, she'd insisted on him purchasing a new black suit. He'd paired it with a white button-up shirt and his brown leather vest this evening, which she found to be a particularly dashing combination.

They made the drive to the inn in silence. As Jesse steered

the horses up the winding gravel drive, he muttered, "Last chance to change your mind, sweetheart."

She reached for his arm. "I think I'd rather just get it over with." Her icy hand warmed against his sun-kissed forearm.

The front door to the inn flew open as Jesse parked the wagon and lifted her down. A woman with a riot of red-gold curls appeared in the doorway. Her gown boasted a waterfall of lacy white ruffles threaded with gossamer gold ribbons. There was no way anyone in this rural mountain town had commissioned such a fine garment, which meant Edward must have ordered it for his wife from back East. Iris's heart gave a momentary twist of envy.

Lacey no longer looked like the penniless woman her former affianced had chosen to marry over her. However, the moment the slender creature glided across the porch, waving a cheerful welcome, Iris's apprehension started to fade. It returned as soon as Edward appeared in the doorway — the perfect aristocrat with his straight shoulders, high forehead, and somber gray eyes.

Iris's anxiety skyrocketed to nearly impossible levels as he scanned her features and went still in recognition. "Iris? Is it really you?" His gaze flew to Jesse. "What's the meaning of this?"

"Yes. Iris and I are married." Jesse's voice was harshly defensive. "It's a long story." He glanced swiftly around them, as if fearing they would be overheard. "One best told indoors."

Lacey managed to maneuver herself so that she was walking by Iris's side as they entered the inn's formal dining room. "Now that we know who you are, I can only imagine how difficult it was for you to accept our invitation to dinner. Regardless, I am glad you came."

"Thank you." Iris hardly knew what else to say, so she kept her silence. In the past, she'd had her wealth, impeccable upbringing, and elevated position in society to bolster her confidence. Nowadays, she simply hoped her gown was clean, and there were no stray chicken feathers stuck in her hair.

"You've certainly changed," Lacey murmured, glancing up and down in approval at Iris's lavender gown.

"How so?"

"For one thing, you look much happier than the first time we met."

"I am," Iris confessed, glancing in the opposite direction to take in the hard set to Jesse's features. It was difficult to read his thoughts, but the way he was hovering made her feel like he was trying to shield her as much as possible from what was coming.

"So Iris has gone and married our Jesse." Lacey's merry smile and tone took some of the tension out of the air. She bustled around the room, waving them into their seats and taking her place beside her husband at the head of the table. "How in the world did you meet?" She leaned forward to clasp her hands on the table. "I can only presume it was during her quick visit to Christmas Mountain a few months ago."

"Like I said, it's a long story." Jesse splayed a hand against Iris's lower back as he guided her into her seat. He bent to speak in her ear. "You don't have to talk about anything you don't want to."

Although she appreciated his efforts to protect her, the fact remained that her former affianced had been an attorney before he'd become an innkeeper. And as much as Iris didn't wish to be beholden to a Remington for anything, she'd been cut off from her money and connections. Perhaps his legal knowledge would serve to balance the scales a bit. At any rate, beggars couldn't be choosers, as the old saying went.

Iris waited until her husband was seated. Then she reached for his hand under the table and started to speak.

"You are correct. We met during my recent visit here with the Remingtons." The memory of her disastrous journey west with Alda and Penn Remington was enough to make her wince. They'd spent the entire train ride piling on the guilt for her failure to maintain Edward's romantic interest in her.

Edward's gray gaze turned curious. "If I correctly recall, your brief encounter ended in a resounding slap to Jesse's face."

Lacey gasped, while Jesse's expression grew thunderous. "It was only for show," he snarled. "Your parents had placed her in an impossible situation. For the record, she apologized before slapping me."

"I did." Iris turned impulsively to her husband, finding strength in his gaze. "The truth is, Jesse had just finished catching me mid-tumble down the stairs. If it wasn't for him, I might have been seriously injured that day." She sighed. "But when Penn Remington glanced our way, I was afraid he would misread Jesse's intentions toward me. Or, worse yet, accuse me of being a woman of loose morals. So I slapped Jesse." She paused and shook her head. "A gesture I regret to this day."

Jesse laced his fingers through hers. "Forget it, Iris. I accepted your apology the moment you gave it."

She gave him a tremulous smile and declared softly, "Even so, I will spend the rest of my days making it up to you."

"You already have." He squeezed her fingers reassuringly. "You gave me everything I ever dreamed of the day you married me."

Edward snorted. "I reckon that means you're a wealthy man now."

Iris hated the way Jesse's shoulders stiffened. "He should be," she hastened to say. "He certainly has every right to my fortune now that we're wed, but we've yet to file a lawsuit to reclaim it."

"What's this about a lawsuit?" Edward demanded. "And why would you need to reclaim anything?"

"That's the part that gets complicated." Jesse went on to describe the way Iris had been assaulted, drugged, and taken on her long journey west. He concluded by saying, "Yes, Iris is the rightful heir to the Hildebrand fortune, but she's not certain it's a battle worth fighting." He shook his head. "Or, quite frankly, one we would stand any real chance of winning."

Edward, who'd been listening in shrewd silence, announced grimly, "You may not have any choice but to fight, my friend."

"I believe that's our decision to make." Iris spoke up stiffly, her cheeks red with suppressed indignation.

With a resigned look, Edward angled his head toward the arched doorway. "May I speak with you alone, Jesse? Man to man?"

Jesse was of the mind to refuse his request and insist whatever he had to say could be said in front of Iris. However, something in Edward's expression stopped him.

With a jerky nod, he rose, stalked from the dining room, and nearly collided with Jack. His next older brother was bearing a silver tray, heaping with pot roast and steamed vegetables. "Leaving so soon?" he muttered, doing a little dance to steady the tray and keep the food from spilling.

"Not at all," Edward assured. "We have a quick matter to discuss, then we'll gladly partake in the feast you've prepared."

Jack quirked an appreciative grin at his boss. "Then I'll be sure to save you a bite or two." To Jesse, he gave a sharp, older brother look. "Jonah's working late this evening on a furniture order. You might want to stop by the carriage house before you leave to let him know you're still alive."

Jesse chuckled and waved two fingers in a mock salute. "If you join us, I'll give you a proper introduction to my wife."

"'Bout time, brother!"

Edward waited until Jack sailed into the dining room with his tray, before unloading what was on his mind. "First and foremost, I am convinced that what Iris's guardian has done to her is downright criminal. That doesn't mean it's going to be easy to prove in a court of law, however."

Jesse grimaced. "Seeing as how we've made it clear we're not inclined to take any legal action—"

"But they will, Jesse." Edward rubbed a hand over the lower half of his face. "The moment they realize she never made it to the asylum, they'll come looking for her."

"How can you be so sure?" Jesse demanded. "They already got what they wanted."

"Because I worked with enough criminals to know how they think. As long as Iris is unaccounted for, she's at the risk of exposing her guardian's scheme. My bet is he'll do every-thing in his power to make sure that doesn't happen."

Jesse raised and lowered his arms. "Do you really think he'd be foolish enough to come after the wife of a deputy?"

"He can't afford not to," Edward retorted grimly. "He won't be calling you by your title of deputy when he does, though. He'll hire someone like my father, who will dig up every speck of dirt there is on you, to include your stint in the asylum. He'll claim it's a matter of one lunatic kidnapping another lunatic. Which means you're going to need a good attorney, yourself."

"He doesn't know I'm involved or where Iris is currently located," Jesse reminded stiffly.

"It won't take him long to connect the dots. Between your stagecoach holdup and the ensuing mail-order marriage contract, all roads will lead to you."

"Then Iris and I will simply have to disappear." Jesse

hated the thought of giving up his new deputy position, but it couldn't be helped. "For good this time."

"Or you could stay and fight what's coming."

"With what?" Jesse possessed a small savings in the bank, but it wasn't nearly enough to retain a lawyer, at least not for long. "I don't have that kind of money."

"You won't need it, because you have me." Edward spread his hands. "It's been a while since I practiced law, but I haven't forgotten my way around a court room."

Jesse snorted. "You'd seriously go head to head against your own father on our behalf?"

"In a heartbeat," Edward growled. "I suspect he's the one behind Fargus Hildebrand's despicable grab for her fortune." His upper lip curled. "Advising him on all the gray areas of the law, including the loopholes, no doubt for a sizable fee."

Jesse gave a low whistle, finding it more difficult than ever to continue despising the innkeeper of Christmas Mountain. "And if we lose our case?"

"I'd rather focus on winning."

"I'm not going back to the asylum, Edward. And over my dead body will anyone cart my wife there."

"So, is that a yes? You'll allow me to represent you and Iris in court?"

Jesse glanced away. "She and I are going to have to think about it first — long and hard."

"Don't think too long," Edward warned. "My guess is that Hildebrand and his cronies are already en route to Texas."

CHAPTER 6: NO REGRETS
JESSE

I ris shot Jesse a concerned look when he returned to the dining room, but he merely returned to his seat beside her and reached for her hand again. He had no wish to discuss anything else about their future in front of Edward and Lacey. Though he very much appreciated Edward's offer to serve as their attorney, launching a lawsuit against Iris's uncle was a decision only he and Iris could make. And he was fairly certain he already knew what his bride's decision on the matter was going to be.

Jack's roast quickly became the next topic of conversation. It had been marinated to perfection with one of his unique cocktails of spices.

Lacey made a humming sound as she took her first bite. "Someday, I'm going to have to wheedle the recipe for this sauce out of you." She leaned over her nephew's baby chair to deposit a few succulent bites of meat on his little plate.

Malachi dove into his dinner with both hands, babbling something unintelligible as he ate. His smile made a dimple appear. Jesse longed to reach across the table and tweak his chubby cheek.

"Sorry, ma'am." Jack passed a bowl of gravy around the table, a teasing smile playing across his aquiline features. "It's a family secret, unless you can get this little fellow to share what he knows." He angled his head at the contentedly chomping toddler. "He's the only one who was allowed to watch me prepare it."

"Oh, my lands, Jack!" Lacey chuckled. "I can only imagine what it would look like, trying to coax a babe into reciting the ingredients to your masterpiece sauces and marinades. No doubt anyone who saw me would presume my wits had gone wandering."

When no one else chuckled at her comment, her lips twisted with regret. "Oh, dear! I reckon that was a poor choice of words, everything considered. Pray forgive me, Jesse. I did not mean to make light of anything you suffered."

"No offense taken, ma'am." He squeezed Iris's hand under the table, and she squeezed back.

Lacey pushed a handful of her riotous curls from her face. "I truly hate what you have suffered as well, Iris, and how you continue to suffer. If there is anything Edward and I can do to help, and I mean anything..."

Iris cocked her head at Jesse, trust shining from her emerald gaze. "Thank you kindly, but my favorite deputy has managed to keep matters well enough in hand, so far. I know we haven't been married for long, but I've seen him talk his way out of some very difficult situations. He'll find us a way out of the current one, too."

"I appreciate your vote of confidence, Mrs. Hawling." In fact, it was something Jesse intended to hang onto with everything he had in him. He brought his wife's hand to his lips. "And now, if you'll excuse us, I promised we'd pay Jonah a visit before we head south to the Crocker farm."

"Be sure to take him some dinner." Lacey hopped to her feet with a birdlike energy and busied herself preparing a plate of food. She draped a clean linen napkin over the top of it and handed it to Iris. "Let him know we missed his company and that we hope he will join us tomorrow evening."

"We sure will, ma'am." Jesse inclined his head respectfully.

"Bah!" Lacey swatted away the hand he held out and stepped closer to give him a quick hug. "You and your brothers have become like family to us, so it would mean a lot if you'd dispense with the titles." She added in a softer voice, "We're going to get through this current muddle, Jesse. One way or the other."

"That's the plan." He returned her hug and stepped back, just in time to catch the strange look Edward was giving Iris.

"Now what?" he muttered, stepping closer to his wife.

Edward continued to regard both of them with something akin to amazement. "Not in a million years did I see this coming."

Jesse's shoulders stiffened at the realization that he considered them to be an incongruous couple.

But before he could form an appropriate retort, Iris's expression slipped back to one of aristocratic hauteur. "Clearly you did not," she agreed coolly. "Otherwise, I would not be in my current predicament." She moved toward the doorway. "However, I forgive you, since you started a chain of events that brought Jesse Hawling into my life, a man whose gallantry knows no bounds." Head held high, she sailed out of the room.

"I reckon I deserved that." Edward stared after her with a regretful twist to his mouth. "Despite her obvious distaste for me, I pray you'll convince her to accept my legal assistance, when the time comes."

"I'll do my best," Jesse replied vaguely, knowing Iris wasn't going to be in favor of accepting help from her former affianced. Not now. Not ever.

He wasn't wrong.

"How can you even suggest such a thing?" Iris gasped only minutes later, when he repeated Edward's offer to serve as their attorney. "Although his refusal to honor our betrothal agreement indirectly contributed to our current happiness, he and his horrid parents are the reason why our freedom is still in jeopardy."

They were gathered in the cozy living area of the carriage house behind the inn. A fire was leaping on the hearth, and Jonah was squatting before it with his plate of leftovers in hand, eagerly devouring the roast his brother had prepared. Jack was standing in front of the window, facing the inn. There was a tension in his tall, wiry frame that made Iris wonder if he was standing guard.

Jesse was sitting beside her on a dark leather sofa, with his arm tossed casually around her shoulders. At her outburst, he'd tugged her closer for a reassuring squeeze.

She gazed anxiously around the room, trying to gauge the expressions of his two brothers. "Maybe it's nothing more than the petty sting of rejection talking, but I don't trust the Remingtons. Not a single one of them, including Edward. Although his offer sounds well meaning on the surface, pray recall that he, too, chose to walk away from his former life in New York. Why am I not justified in doing the same?"

"Good point." Her hulking oldest brother-in-law sent a crooked smile in her direction before tackling his last slice of roast.

She appreciated his quick verbal leap to her defense. "Thank you." She glanced around the newly renovated carriage house. "That said, it will not offend me if you feel differently. It certainly appears as if Edward has turned over a new leaf. All around us is proof of the many things he and

Lacey are doing to improve the lives of others, which I find admirable."

"I reckon he's done a decent number of things to improve our community, as a whole." Jesse shrugged. "After showing up at the eleventh hour to thwart our plans to jump a claim on the inn property. Sometimes, I wonder if he befriended and hired us Hawlings more out of guilt than anything else."

Jack, who'd been staring into the distance through the front window, chimed in to the conversation at this point. "Although you have every right to be angry with him, Iris, I've worked closely with him for the past several months, and this I can honestly say. He genuinely despises his former life. Most unfortunately, you were part of that life."

"I could say the same," she retorted. "He, too, was once part of a life I wish to shed." She pursed her lips. "So I most definitely do not need his assistance in being restored to it." A burst of emotion made her voice hitch. "What you have here..." She spread her hands. "Not the carriage house, but your brotherhood, is priceless. Which reminds me." She gave the three men a trembly smile. "I haven't yet properly thanked you for my rescue. The risks you took upon yourselves to remove me from that dratted stagecoach were tremendous. I shall not soon forget it."

Jonah turned an abashed shade of red. "Aw, it was nothing much."

"He's right." Jack nodded, grinning. "All we really had to do was stay out of firing range."

"You're only being modest," she chided. "No matter how you try to downplay what you did, I know it was your bravery and selflessness that kept me a free woman." She couldn't fathom what it would have been like to be confined to an asylum cell, though she suspected it would've felt much like a prison.

Jonah gave a nonchalant shrug. "That's what family is for,

Iris. You became a member of ours the moment Jesse married you."

"And you came, no questions asked, when he called you?" She couldn't have been more moved by the brothers' loyalty to each other.

"Sure did," Jack agreed, though he shook a finger at her, scowling ferociously. "Even so, we wouldn't have minded an invitation to the wedding. If Jesse had warned us you were going to get hitched the same afternoon, I would've at least baked a cake to celebrate the occasion."

Iris blinked back the sting of happy tears. "Maybe you could still bake us that cake sometime?" she asked hopefully. "After we put the current crisis behind us, of course."

"Speaking of our current crisis." Jesse lightly drummed his fingers against her upper arm. "Are we all in agreement, then, that Iris and I will not be accepting Edward's offer to serve as our attorney?"

Iris nodded vehemently. "I want a clean and solid break from everything I left behind in New York, and that means no legal battles with my uncle. According to our dear benefactor, Mr. Crocker, if my uncle continues to live by thievery and trickery, my former wealth will be nothing but a curse to him, anyway."

"Amen and pass the bacon!" Jonah teased. "Sounds like somebody got religion."

"Not exactly." She blushed. "He's just been around a while and has plenty of wisdom to share."

"If you're certain this is what both of you want, then you have my support," Jack crossed his arms, looking pensive, "which means we need to come up with an escape plan for the two of you."

Iris blinked at Jesse in bewilderment. "Escape?"

He nodded gravely. "Too many folks already know about your arrival in Christmas Mountain. The minister, Clink

Redwood, and the Remingtons, to name a few. I wouldn't be surprised if word has gotten around about how we've been staying with Old Man Crocker, too."

Jonah set his empty plate on the hearth and straightened, stretching his back to work out a kink. "So, what are our best options? Any caves on the property, storm shelters, or the like?"

"Not that I'm aware of." Jesse shook his head. "Even if there was, I'd like something a little more sure-fire than that."

Jack spun around slowly. "Christmas Mountain Inn is located on the north side of town. The Crocker homestead is due south of here. But has anyone considered what's east of both places?"

"Now we're talking." Jesse dropped his arms from Iris's shoulders and sat forward in excitement.

Iris had no idea what they were talking about. "Would someone please tell me what lies to the east of us?" She was suddenly dying to know.

"Comanches." Jesse dropped his voice and uttered the word in a ghostly whisper.

She unconsciously lifted a hand to her hair, eliciting a round of male chuckles from the brothers. "I'd dearly love to keep my scalp intact, if it's all the same to you gentlemen."

Jesse winked at her. "Never fear. I'm rather fond of your lovely scalp, as well, Mrs. Hawling."

"So I've truly arrived in the Wild West," she murmured, her heart thumping with trepidation. "Are there really Comanches living up in the mountains?"

Jesse made a scoffing sound. "I'm far more concerned about the savages in New York, than I am of a few Natives living up on Christmas Mountain."

Jonah drew his dark brows together. "I'd be more in agreement, if Chief Pecos and I hadn't been locked in such a fiery dispute over property lines in recent months. He doesn't exactly strike me as a forgive and forget sort of fellow."

"That doesn't sound good." Iris glanced worriedly between the brothers. "Was your dispute ever resolved?"

"As a matter of fact, yes." Jack waggled his brows. "A certain attorney turned innkeeper used his powers of negotiation to bring about the cease fire. In return, he promised to help keep all would-be gold prospectors off the mountain. Once upon a time, we were nearly overrun with the get-rich-quick crowd. They were forever blowing through the caverns and caves with dynamite. Liked to about destabilized the entire area we're standing on."

"The dynamite explosions were also scattering the wild mustang herds to the four winds," Jesse added. "Since Chief Pecos is in the business of taming and selling them to ranchers all over the region, that was a big problem for him. From what I've heard, he's quite the enterprising business-man, which gives me an idea. I'll have to run it past Mr. Crocker, of course, but I suspect Pecos would jump at the chance to access a set of stables and prime grazing land on the south side of town." His dark gaze grew calculating. "I was thinking we could offer to board and showcase his horses to prospective buyers, and possibly even handle the sales transactions."

"For a fee, of course," Jonah interjected.

"Naturally." Jesse nodded.

"If we successfully increase his profit margin, I reckon our past dispute wouldn't matter near as much," Jonah mused.

"That's the plan." Jesse leaned his forearms on his knees, tapping his fingertips together. "The real question is, how far would he go to protect the lives of his business partners? He might not own much in the way of grazing land, but he and his Comanches know a thing or two about fading into their environment. They're the kind of folk who can't be found unless they want to be found."

Iris caught her lower lip between her teeth. "If you're referring to living in caves and wearing next to nothing in the way of clothing..." Her eyes grew round in horrified contemplation.

"Nothing that drastic, sweetheart." Jesse's gaze twinkled into hers as he stood. "Though it does get hot here in the summers, I've never once had the hankering to strip down to a loincloth." He reached for her hand.

She blushed a deep shade of pink as she placed her hand in his.

"Nor have I." Jonah chortled as he watched the tender way Jesse tugged his bride to her feet.

"Gee, thanks." Jack rolled his eyes. "That's a mental picture I could've gladly lived without." He pretended to stomp in high dudgeon from the room. However, he returned a few minutes later with a picnic basket, brimming with fresh-baked bread and several jars of homemade honey butter. He presented it to Jesse and Iris with a flourish. "I'd be much obliged if you'd carry this to Old Man Crocker. It's my way of saying thank you for the way he's opened his home to you."

Iris reached for the handle. "He will be delighted, I assure you. The poor fellow has no family left, unless you count a few old barn cats that might actually have been around longer than he has."

Jonah nodded in approval. "If you don't mind lingering another minute or two, I might have something to add to the pile." He lumbered up the stairs to his bedchamber and returned with a sturdy oak cane. It had a beautifully tooled horse's head for a handle.

Iris's striking green eyes rounded in wonder. "You actually made this?"

"Did he ever!" Jack spread his hands proudly. "Everything fashioned of wood in this room is his handiwork."

Knowing that Iris probably knew a thing or two about finely crafted furniture from all over the world, Jesse watched her closely as she took a moment to survey the carriage house living room as closely as she had when they'd first entered it. She drank in the beauty of the intricately carved eagle resting on the mantle over the fireplace, the pair of raw edge pine wood end tables, and the twisted rattler candlestick holders resting atop them.

"You have a real gift, Jonah," she said simply.

Jonah's dark gaze glinted with pride at her gracious approval as he handed over the cane.

Jesse accepted his brother's gift with a smile. "Old Man Crocker will appreciate this every bit as much as the bread. He has a difficult time getting around some days, holding on to walls, railings, and such. He tries his hardest to pretend otherwise, blaming the dogs for stepping in his path. But we all know it's just his rheumatism acting up."

⚜

ON THE TRIP BACK TO THE FARM, IRIS WAS GIDDY WITH happiness. "Your brothers are amazing," she gushed. "One can cook like a god, and the other could probably whittle a whole castle, given enough time."

"Then there's me." Jesse cuddled her closer on the wagon seat, no easy task while holding the reins to his borrowed team of horses.

"And then there's you," she echoed softly. Her breath clogged in her throat at the answering smolder in his dark gaze.

"Any regrets about marrying me?" he inquired softly.

"None," she assured. "You've given me everything I've

ever dreamed of. Family. Adventure." She glanced pointedly down at her precious burdens. "And fresh-baked bread."

"Adventure?" He waggled his brows at her. "I reckon that's one way of putting it."

She smiled. "Most importantly, you've given me you." Her smile became strained. "I should probably ask you the same question. Do you have any regrets about marrying me, Jesse? I know I was supposed to come with a lot more money and—"

He stopped her by leaning closer for a kiss. "No."

"We might never be wealthy at the rate we're going," she sighed.

"Still no regrets." He brushed his lips against hers again.

"If we have to go on the run, you could even lose your job." Her voice grew shaky.

His gaze burned into hers. "You're more important to me than a dusty old badge, Iris. The sheriff mostly uses me as his errand boy, anyway. He might actually learn to appreciate me if he has to do without my assistance for a few days."

Her eyes grew damp. "You're just saying that to try to make me feel better, aren't you?"

"It depends." He tweaked one of the curls against her cheek. "Is it working?"

"Yes." She couldn't wait until they were alone, so she could show him exactly how much his efforts were working.

CHAPTER 7: RUMBLINGS OF TROUBLE

IRIS

The packed dirt road leading to Old Man Crocker's homestead was washed out in several places, so Jesse had to carefully maneuver the horse-drawn wagon around the most unstable spots.

The red-gold streaks of sunset were fading to darker hues of purple and blue. A rumble of thunder in the distance was Iris's first clue that the fast deepening shadows portended something other than the coming night.

"Use those sharp, eagle eyes of yours," her husband muttered to the horses. "We're almost there, but you're still carrying precious cargo."

"By the way, what's your Palomino's name?" she asked curiously, realizing she'd never heard him use it. "I've been meaning to ask."

"Butler." Though a cloud passed over the moon, pitching them into near blackness, she could hear the smile in her husband's voice.

She angled her head at him to catch his eye. "Dare I ask why?"

"I was but sixteen when I acquired him, and beyond

weary of being the youngest brother in the pecking order. For all intents and purposes, I named him Butler, just so I could finally have a turn at bossing someone else around."

She dissolved into giggles. "Say it isn't so."

"I could, but it wouldn't change the truth." His voice was sheepish.

She laughed harder.

"Hush, sweetheart!" He abruptly reached up to cup a hand over her mouth.

She instantly grew still, wondering what was amiss.

"Something isn't right," he whispered against her ear. He slowed the horses to a walk and eased them off the road into the scrubby grasses to help muffle the sound of their hooves.

It suddenly dawned on Iris that they should have been able to see a light by now. Mr. Crocker was so kind and fatherly, he would have surely kept a lantern burning in a window for them. Unless, of course, something had prevented him from doing so.

Her heart thumped with dread as they clip-clopped closer to the dark windows of the farmhouse.

"Shh!" Jesse whispered, lowering his hand from her mouth. He parked the wagon at the far end of the veranda and leaped silently to the ground to secure the horses. Then he reached up to assist Iris. Pressing his lips to her ear, he instructed, "Stay behind me, darlin'."

They crept along the length of the porch to the stairs.

"Come another step, and I'll blow your head off!" a man called so hoarsely that it took Iris an extra second to recognize it as belonging to their fearless host.

"Mr. Crocker?" she gasped, dashing around her husband toward the stairs.

"I thought I told you to stay behind me," he grumbled, following her.

"Oh, thank heavens it's you!" the old farmer sighed, sounding close to weeping. "I thought they'd come back."

The snarling clouds overhead shifted, allowing a shaft of pale moonlight through. It was enough to illuminate Mr. Crocker's knobby limbs. He was sprawled on the porch floor, clutching his rifle while leaning back against the front door.

"Who was here?" Jesse demanded, running forward to drop to one knee beside him.

Iris set down the gifts from Jesse's brothers on the edge of the porch, so she could join them. Crouching down on Mr. Crocker's other side, she surveyed him in concern, hoping he wasn't injured.

"Not sure who they were. There were two of them, though. Came galloping straight up the road on a pair of half-wild mustangs with their faces half covered like bandits. They were demanding an audience with you, son."

"Interesting." Jesse's gaze narrowed. "Did they say who they were?"

"No, and I didn't ask. Just told them I lived alone. The younger one got mouthy after that, so I told them to get off my property before I plugged their shirts full of holes. Then I shot over their heads to send their horses running."

"How long ago was this?" Jesse squinted into the darkness, as if searching for any more signs of trouble.

"An hour, I'd say."

"Have you been sitting outside, keeping watch ever since?" It seemed to Iris that he'd have been much safer waiting inside.

"In a matter of speaking." Mr. Crocker rolled to one hip and tried to stand, but had to bite back a groan. "It's been a while since I shot this rifle, and I'd all but forgotten what a powerful kick it has. Liked to knock me plumb off my feet."

Iris's stricken gaze met Jesse's. They knew it was his quirky way of admitting he'd fallen.

"Alright, then." Jesse leaned closer to loop Mr. Crocker's arm over his own shoulder. "Let's get you inside, shall we?" He slowly rose to his feet, easily bearing the weight of the older gentleman.

Mr. Crocker wasn't able to put any weight on his left foot without groaning.

"Looks like you've injured your ankle, sir." As Jesse prepared to lift him in his arms, Iris shook her head vehemently. Mr. Crocker's stubborn pride could only bear so much.

Nodding in understanding, Jesse waited while she moved to the edge of the porch to snatch up Jonah's gift.

"Here." She handed Mr. Crocker the sturdy oak cane with its ornately carved handle. "It's a gift from Jesse's oldest brother, Jonah. He wanted to thank you for your kindness in allowing us to stay here with you."

"Well, I'll be!" Looking pleased beyond belief, Mr. Crocker reached for the stick and used it to finish hobbling across the threshold with Jesse's assistance.

"There." Jesse deposited him in his favorite high-back chair with a cushion near the fireplace. "How about taking a load off your feet for a bit?"

Mr. Crocker settled against the cushion. "This does feel a mite better than that hard floor outside." His grateful gaze settled on Jesse. "But it sure did give me time to appreciate all the work you've done to the front porch. Not too long ago, the roof was about to fall in, and there was dry rot everywhere. It looks like a whole new porch now."

"Well, you can thank my oldest brother for that, too." In that moment, it was clear to Iris how much Jesse admired Jonah's construction skills. "He taught me everything I know about how to hold a hammer and nails."

"I sure will, first chance I get," Mr. Crocker promised with a decided nod.

Iris turned on the lantern resting atop the narrow end table next to his chair. A warm, golden glow filled the living room.

"Glory be, but you're a sight for sore eyes! Both of you." Mr. Crocker watched in humble appreciation as Jesse remained stooped to remove his boots.

"I apologize if this hurts, but we'd best get them off before the swelling gets worse." Jesse peeled off his sock, then ran his thumbs across the bridge of his foot. "Doesn't appear to be broken. That's good. But your ankle does feel a bit swollen. My guess is, you sprained it."

"Well, it's not my first injury, and it probably won't be the last." Old Man Crocker surveyed his puffy ankle in irritation. "I'm not as limber as I used to be."

"Well, you don't have to be, now that you have us," Iris soothed. She ran back outside to fetch the picnic basket from Jack and returned with it in her arms. "Look what Jack Hawling sent you!"

He gave a tentative sniff. "Smells like fresh-baked bread."

"Plus honey butter." Over the top of the basket, she cocked her head at him. "Would you care for a slice?"

"Make it two." He gave her a rueful grin. "Between my unexpected visitors and my near tumble down the stairs, I missed my dinner."

"Coming right up." She moved into the kitchen with the basket and returned a few minutes later with a platter. She'd carefully arranged about half a loaf's worth of slices in a semi-circle around a jar of the honey butter. Delivering the platter to the same side table where the lantern rested, she announced in a merry voice, "Dinner is served."

In the short time she'd been out of the room, Jesse had wrapped Mr. Crocker's injured ankle. He rocked back on his heels to survey the bandage. "That should hold."

"You're an answer to my prayers," Mr. Crocker

announced, thumping his new cane on the floor for emphasis, "both of you."

Iris smiled. "Well, Jesse was the answer to my prayers before he was the answer to yours. It seems as if the good Lord has seen fit to pass his gallantry around a bit lately."

To her surprise, Mr. Crocker broke into a loud guffaw, slapping his knee a few times.

She blinked. "Did I say something funny, sir?"

"To me, you did," he chortled. "I reckon you'd have to know the senior Mr. Hawling the way I do, to find any humor in that statement."

Jesse's dark brows lifted. "You know my father, sir?"

"That I do." Mr. Crocker sniffed. "I visit him every week on Monday like clockwork. Sheriff Dawson learnt a long time ago not to question my coming and going."

"I'm sure he appreciates your visits." The tone of Jesse's voice hinted that his father might not get too many other visitors.

Iris didn't know much about Jesse's father, other than the fact that he was most sadly behind bars.

Mr. Crocker pursed his lips as if tasting something bitter. "It's a crying shame they locked him up on the testimony of a drunkard."

Jesse went still. "Would you mind saying that again, sir?"

"I shouldn't, since I gave my word to your pa that I wouldn't talk about his incarceration to you boys." The older man's gaze became unfocused as his mind drifted to more distant memories. "Figured he would've told you the truth by now, though."

"Which is what, exactly?" Jesse scowled for reasons Iris didn't understand.

"I reckon it wouldn't hurt for you to hear a few things after all this time," Mr. Crocker sighed. "Now that yer ma's gone, I'm not sure why yer pa insists on keepin' everything so bottled up."

JESSE STOOD, CLENCHING HIS FISTS AS HE WAITED FOR HIM to continue his story.

"It was ol' Ike Remington up to his usual tricks. He started off by cheatin' in cards, which forced yer pa to keep his end of their bet and cancel his purchase contract on the land they both wanted. He always swore yer pa wouldn't have been able to afford it, anyway, but who knows? Not too long after, Ike's drunken front desk clerk at the inn testified against yer pa in court, claiming he saw 'em slaughter a fella in cold blood over an insult to yer ma. There weren't no truth to it, though, 'cause the coroner later claimed the scallawag died from a bullet in his chest. Yer pa wasn't even armed at the time." He shook his head in disgust. "I'm madder than a hornet all over again, just thinkin' about it!"

For a moment, Jesse couldn't see past the blood in his eyes. Way down in his heart, he'd always suspected his pa had been framed for a crime he hadn't committed, and now he had confirmation of it.

That's it. I'm gonna pay a visit to the jail, come morning, and I'm demanding the truth at last. If his father was truly innocent of the crime he'd been accused of, Jesse might very well accept Edward's offer for legal representation, after all. It was the least Edward could do to make amends for his family's many wrongs.

As soon as Jesse could get Mr. Crocker's feet propped on a stool and his knees covered with a blanket, he angled his head at Iris, silently begging her to follow him to their bedchamber. Shutting the door behind him, he leaned against it and drew her into his arms.

"It's been a long day, hasn't it?" He cuddled her close, needing her sweetness and warmth to chase away the darkness gathering in his heart.

"Yes, but we're going to get through this mess, Jesse." She hugged him back tightly. "I just know we are."

"How can you be so sure?" He gazed bleakly over her shoulder at the rustic bed piled with patchwork quilts. Like everything else in Old Man Crocker's home, the furnishings inside his spare room were old and faded, but clean. He and Iris could've been happy here for a long time to come. She adored living in the country. However, it was beginning to look as if their idyllic existence on the farm was about to be cut short.

"Because of how many of my prayers have been answered lately." She leaned back in his arms to tip her classically oval face up to his. "Starting with the one I prayed at least a thousand times on my way from New York to Texas. I begged the Lord to allow my plea for help to reach you."

Despite the direness of their circumstances, he couldn't help being amazed all over again by how beautiful his wife was, on both the inside and the outside. She wasn't just attractive, either; she was downright stunning — an angelic blonde with perfect porcelain features.

He watched the play of emotions across her fine-boned face, utterly besotted by the adoration he read there. "Even if it's true that Divine Providence used me to answer a few of your prayers, it's possible the worst is still yet to come. I can only presume those two fellows Old Man Crocker fired at were some of the thugs your uncle sent after us."

She slid her arms around his neck. "But why would the Lord save me from the frying pan, only to throw me into the fire? It just doesn't add up."

"Sweetheart, there's nothing right about the many injustices that have been meted out to both your family and mine." Despite how differently the two of them had been raised, they'd certainly found common ground in their recent suffering.

"True, but an awful lot of good has come into our lives, along with the bad. You, for instance. I have you, Jesse."

He leaned in to bump noses with her. "You're an incurable optimist, aren't you?"

"I mean it, Jesse. I was the most miserable woman alive before I met you. I would trade my wealth all over again to be right here in your arms."

"With a set of paid mercenaries dogging our heels, etc?" he teased.

"Yes." She stood on her tiptoes to brush her lips against his. "I would trade my wealth to be with you, no matter what."

For a moment, regret slammed into him at how content she was with so little. "This is far from the life I'd planned for us, darlin'. Far from the life you deserve."

"And yet I've never been happier." She kissed him again.

"Me, neither," he confessed in a voice rough with emotion. Taking what she offered, he deepened their kiss and allowed the light in her to chase away the darkness.

❧

HE WAITED UNTIL SHE WAS CURLED SNUGLY BENEATH THE blankets on their bed, her breathing soft and even in sleep, before he carried out the next part of his plan.

Dressing quickly, he padded down the hallway in his sock feet and tiptoed across the living room toward the front door. Or tried to.

Old Man Crocker's voice stopped him. "Need I remind you that purty little wife of yers is dependin' on you to stay in one piece, son?"

Jesse paused, knowing that their kind host deserved some sort of explanation for why he was sneaking out of the house so late at night. "I don't plan on doing anything foolish, sir. I'm only trying to protect her. To protect all of us."

"And how do you plan on doin' that?"

"By paying a visit to our neighbors from the east. I'd like to negotiate a business arrangement, if it's alright with you." With a little luck, he'd make it onto the Comanche reservation without having his person peppered with arrows like a pincushion.

"In the middle of the night?"

Jesse shrugged. "Seems like we don't have much time to waste, considering the surprise visit from those thugs earlier."

"I reckon I cain't deny that." Mr. Crocker gripped his rifle more tightly against his shoulder. Moonlight poured through the window, making him look like a ghostly soldier. "What sorta business arrangement?"

Jesse made a rueful face. "Putting your barns and pastures back to use, if you're willing. I'd like to offer to board the Comanche mustangs here and showcase them to prospective buyers. If we do it right, we could turn you a tidy profit. Plus, it would allow me to finally earn my keep here."

Mr. Crocker gave a long, low whistle. "You're an enterprising fool, ain't ya?"

"I've been called worse."

"I reckon making the Comanches yer allies would give you and that sweet wife of yers a place to hide without having to run too far."

"That's the bigger plan, sir."

His host looked vastly approving. "Assuming there's no talking you out of yer plan, you'd best learn the secret password. Otherwise you might not live long enough to gain an audience with Chief Pecos."

"There's a secret password?" Jesse was amused, despite the gravity of the situation.

"Of course there is. How else do you think I survived this long on my own?"

As it turned out, the "secret password" wasn't a password at all; it was a signal, one that would require a blazing lantern when Jesse reached his final destination.

"I don't know how to thank you, sir." He was overwhelmed with gratitude by the continued generosity of his host.

"Just get back here alive, ya here? That's all the thanks I need."

Nodding, Jesse headed outside into the darkness. Once he reached the porch, he stepped into his boots. The sky was still festering with clouds, but the storm he thought was heading their way earlier seemed to be passing them by. Nothing more than a few scattered raindrops glanced off his cheeks as he untethered the horses.

"You probably wondered what was taking me so long, eh?" Jesse led them to the barnyard, so they could drink their fill of water and munch on hay before he set out again. This time, he saddled his Palomino.

Butler nickered in excitement as they prepared to hit the trail together. Jesse refilled his canteen and tied a rolled blanket behind his saddle, should he end up needing to pitch a bed under the open skies tonight.

Then he leaped into the saddle and took off. Since his horse was so well trained, Jesse set nothing more than their general direction. He allowed Butler to set his own pace and to choose the best trail through the darkened foothills.

A coyote howled in the distance, but another rumble of thunder silenced him. Jesse rode until he reached the highest peak between Old Man Crocker's property and the reservation. Then he did as he'd been instructed. Lighting the lantern he'd brought with him, he waved his Stetson back and forth in front of it. He gave three passes of his hat before holding it steady in front of the lantern. Waiting approximately a minute, he repeated the sequence. After nearly a dozen attempts at signaling the Comanche chief, he doused the flame. Settling in his saddle, he wondered if such a rudimentary form of communication would even be seen by their Native neighbors, much less acted on.

He lingered a good half hour or more, squinting through the darkness while trying to discern any sign of human activity ahead. There was none. Sucking in a disappointed breath, he finally started to wheel his horse around. However, the snap of a twig made him pause.

"Is anyone there?" he called out softly.

The hard, round barrel of a rifle was pressed between his shoulder blades. "Raise your hands in the air. No sudden moves or else."

It took a superhuman effort for Jesse not to reach for his pistols and try to shoot his way out of whatever trouble he'd stumbled into. However, all he could think of were Iris's words from earlier.

Why would the good Lord save me from the frying pan, only to throw me into the fire?

Though it went against his normal grain, Jesse decided to take a leap of faith by raising his hands in the air.

He was summarily relieved of both his guns, plus the blade he kept stowed inside his boot.

"Now ride," the voice commanded. "Due east. The chief is expecting you."

Jesse's shoulders relaxed. He's been right to cooperate with the faceless voice. Everything was falling into its proper place, just as Iris had predicted. *She'll be happy to hear another prayer has been answered.* The thought made him smile into the darkness.

Picking up his reins, he nudged his knees into Butler's flanks. "Let's go, old boy."

About a mile up the mountain, they rode into a clearing dotted with rustic little shacks. A bonfire burned at the center of it, and the man Jesse sought was standing directly before it.

The flickering firelight outlined Chief Pecos's distinctively Native garb, a fur cloak over a pair of fringed deerskin trousers. His long, dark hair hung loosely down his back, though a few strands whipped across his angular face in the mountain breeze.

Arms crossed, he addressed Jesse as he rode nearer. "It's been many moons since the Comanches have been called by way of the lantern. What trouble brings you our way?"

CHAPTER 8: TRICKY NEGOTIATION

JESSE

"Some very bad *hombres*," Jesse supplied curtly. "They threatened Old Man Crocker earlier today, but I have reason to believe that my wife and I are their real targets."

"Come." Chief Pecos unfolded his arms and waved at Jesse to join him by the fire.

The moment Jesse leaped to the ground, hands reached for the reins of his horse.

"Do not fear. Your horse will be well cared for." The chief beckoned again for Jesse to join him.

"And my weapons?" he inquired as he strode in the man's direction.

"They'll be returned to you when you exit our camp."

"Fair enough." Jesse nodded. Though he didn't like being disarmed, he understood the reasons behind such a precautionary gesture. "I came to present a business proposal that I believe will greatly benefit you and your people, at least in terms of money."

Chief Pecos's expression didn't change, though his dark eyes flashed with curiosity. "If it is business you wish to discuss, it is the way of my people to share a ceremonial pipe before we begin negotiations." The hard line of his mouth turned down in a grimace. "Especially since you're kin to a man we've traded way too many bullets with, in recent months."

Jesse shook his head in disgust. Jonah was shamefully bull-headed when it came to defending the blasted fence line between the reservation and Christmas Mountain Inn. "I'm sorry for the trouble my brother has caused you. I trust he never injured anyone? Physically, that is?"

"No." Chief Pecos reached inside a pouch strapped to his side and produced a long ceremonial pipe. "He wasn't aiming for us. Never did more than shoot over our heads, though it was a powerful annoyance to the mustangs."

"Well, it won't happen again." *I hope. Only time will tell.*

"That is what the innkeeper has promised." Chief Pecos stuffed a pinch of tobacco inside the pipe, lit it, and puffed for a few seconds. "By this pipe, I pledge to participate in a peaceful negotiation." He gave it one last puff before handing it over.

Jesse had no idea what was expected of him in the hoodoo-voodoo Native ceremony, but he inwardly vowed to give it his best shot. "I come in peace and hope to leave here as your friend and ally." *Preferably with a solid escape plan in place, should it come to that.* He gave a light puff on the pipe without inhaling very deeply. Unaccustomed to smoking tobacco, he didn't wish to embarrass himself by coughing or wheezing from the smoke and fumes. Handing the pipe back to Chief Pecos, he waited, hoping he'd done it right.

"I am now ready to hear your offer."

I'll take that as a yes on my successful pipe twirling. Jesse smoth-ered the grin that tugged at the edges of his mouth. "We'd like to work out an agreement to board your saddle-broke mustangs in Old Man Crocker's barns. For a small fee, of course. It takes money to feed and water horses. For that same fee, we'll also show the horses to prospective buyers and assist with the paperwork during the final sales transaction." He could consult Edward Remington about the proper documentation for the legal transfer of ownership between horse owners.

Chief Pecos studied him intently. "Seems to me that a sales commission might also be prudent. Otherwise, you'd have no inclination to turn over my herd."

Jesse nodded. He hadn't wanted to press for too much too soon, but he'd been hoping in that direction.

"If I agree to a business partnership, what was the purpose of tonight's distress signal?"

Jesse spread his hands, ready to plead his case. "My wife and I might need to disappear for a while."

"Why is that?" Chief Pecos looked vastly intrigued.

"There's a distinct chance those bad hombres I mentioned earlier will come back. My wife is the heir to a fortune, you see. Unfortunately, her guardian recently tried to have her committed to an insane asylum, in the hopes of gaining full control of it. He'd like me out of the way, as well, since my legal claim to that same fortune outweighed his the day I married his niece."

Chief Pecos dumped the final remnants of tobacco from his pipe into the fire. Then he returned the ceremonial pipe to his pouch. "So you'll take him to the white man's court and become a wealthy man."

"Not exactly," Jesse sighed, lifting his hat to run a hand through his hair. "My wife considers the money to be cursed and has no wish to return to her former life. She'd rather remain on Old Man Crocker's farm, naming the cows and gathering chicken eggs."

Amusement flickered in the dark gaze of his listener. "I am beginning to see the problem."

"Indeed. Alas, our plans to remain in the country won't keep her uncle from coming after us. So long as we're living free, we're a threat to his criminal activities."

Chief Pecos's expression grew cagey. "My people can make it so that no man will ever find you again, unless you wish to be found. But, in your absence, who will board my mustangs and show them to prospective buyers?"

"I have two brothers."

"One I have no wish to do business with."

"Fine." Jesse's lips twitched at the realization that the Comanche chief was like a fish that had been thoroughly caught. It was only a matter of reeling him in. "Jonah can put his itchy trigger fingers to work mucking out stalls. The only one you'll have to deal with in my absence, if it comes to that, is Jack. I give you my word." He held out a hand to shake on it.

Chief Pecos left Jesse's arm extended in mid-air so long that he began to doubt they had a deal, after all. However, he resisted the urge to fidget or shift his weight from one boot to the other. Instead, he continued to squarely meet the chief's gaze. He had nothing to hide, a fact he was counting on Pecos deducing for himself.

His eyes started to burn from the need to blink more often.

Then, without so much as a twitch of his facial muscles, Chief Pecos reached out to clasp Jesse's wrist.

Jesse closed his hand around the chief's arm in return, locking them hand-to-wrist. They spent the next several minutes negotiating the terms of their agreement — from boarding prices to a commission on each horse sale. Both bargained hard, but both also conceded a few demands in order to come to a satisfactory agreement. It gave Jesse a favorable impression of what it would be like to work with Chief Pecos in the coming days.

To conclude their meeting, Jesse drawled, "I certainly hope I never have to take you up on your offer to make my wife and me disappear. If it happens, however, we'll continue to work from the shadows."

Chief Pecos nodded. "We have a deal, Deputy." He unclasped Jesse's wrist and dropped his hand back to his side.

Jesse continued to hold the man's gaze. "I'll be ready for your first delivery of mustangs on the morrow."

"And you shall have them." Looking supremely pleased with his end of the bargain, Chief Pecos extended one arm west. "Head back in the direction you came from. One of my tribesmen will be at the perimeter to return your weapons."

Jesse rode back to the Crocker homestead in the wee hours of the morning. After circling the farmhouse a few times to ensure there were no unwelcome intruders lying in wait for him, he returned Butler to the stables for some well-deserved tending and rest. Then he strode silently up the stairs of the farmhouse porch. Either Old Man Crocker was asleep when he crept through the living room, or he was pretending to be. Whichever the case, Jesse made it back to his bedchamber without any more cross-examinations, for which he was supremely grateful.

The euphoria of his successful business arrangement with the Comanches was starting to fade into exhaustion. After freshening up a bit, he gingerly rolled onto his side of the bed, trying not to disturb his slumbering bride. However, the moment he laid back against the pillows, she shifted in his direction.

"You're back," she murmured sleepily, lifting her head to drop it on his shoulder. "In the morning, you can tell me all about it."

He kissed the top of her head, breathing in her clean, soapy scent. "I will," he promised against her temple.

"I love you, Jesse," she whispered. "So much."

He froze, hardly able to believe his ears. For many days, he'd been hoping for such a miracle, not quite dreaming that a man of his humble beginnings would ever get to experience such bliss. "Iris, honey," he muttered huskily, cuddling her closer.

But there was no answer. Her breathing had already evened back into sleep.

Alas, sleep evaded Jesse for a long time. *My wife loves me.* Deep in his heart, he'd always known that she cared, but there was nothing quite like hearing the words and gaining proof of her affections.

The only thing shadowing his joy, was the fear that she might not remember saying the words tomorrow. Or, worse yet, she might no longer feel like saying them after she found out what he was planning next.

CHAPTER 9: LAST STAND

IRIS

A blast of sunlight warmed Iris's face, jostling her awake. *Oh, my lands!* She felt as lazy as a cat with a belly full of cream. Or, in the case of Mr. Crocker's barn cats, a belly full of squirrel or pigeon.

It was a good thing it was the weekend. Though Jesse could get summoned to work at any point, he generally didn't put in a full day of work at the sheriff's office on Saturdays. He generally stayed home for breakfast and went in later.

She stretched out a hand to his side of the bed and felt nothing but air. Eyelids snapping open, she found herself staring directly at the antique wardrobe they were sharing, which meant she was already lying on Jesse's side of the bed. It additionally meant he'd already risen, dressed, and left their bedchamber.

Disappointment crashed through her as she sat up, along with the last fragments of a dark and fuzzy memory. He'd returned to bed in the middle of the night. She was certain of it. She could recall cuddling up to him and telling him... She caught her breath. *Did I really tell him that I love him?*

Most unfortunately, she couldn't remember him saying it

back, though he'd whispered her name and nuzzled her temple with devastating tenderness. She couldn't recall anything that had happened next. Or, if it had even happened at all...

Moaning aloud, Iris threw her legs over the side of the bed, wondering why she'd slept so long. It was well past daybreak. No wonder Jesse was absent. He always rose with the sun to get started on the biggest chores around the farm.

As she stood, a powerful wave of dizziness struck her, making her plop back on the edge of the bed. *What is wrong with me? Am I falling ill?* She pressed a hand to her forehead and was relieved to discover she didn't feel feverish. In fact, the strange wave of dizziness was quickly abating.

Though she wasn't normally given to bouts of nausea, maybe she was simply hungry or thirsty. Or maybe she was still tired. It had been a long, stressful night with Jesse absent from bed for so long. She really hadn't rested much until he returned home. Wondering where he had been, she rose to her feet once again to go ask him for herself.

"Oh-h-h-h-h!" She sucked in a breath as another wave of the strange dizziness rocked her nearly off her feet. "My lands!" She laid a hand on the bed for support, panting through the worst of it until her balance was restored.

And then she knew what was wrong.

I am about to become a mother! It's the only explanation that made sense for a woman exhibiting no other obvious signs of illness. *I'm going to have a baby!* Jesse's baby. Just as they'd hoped, their little family was growing.

Getting dressed for the day turned out to be one of the most difficult tasks Iris had ever tackled. She had to keep pausing and fanning her face to make the odd feelings pass long enough to don her dress and style her hair. Because she had such wonderful news to tell her husband, she took extra care with her appearance, selecting the blue cotton gown he'd specially commissioned for her.

The dress was a far cry from the elegant wardrobe she'd owned back in New York. It was a simple, pale blue cotton, nearly white, dotted with tiny embroidered pink rosettes. He'd purchased her an embroidered collar and a sash to wear with it, both in a shade of darker blue. The ensemble was far from exotic; nevertheless, she thought she looked fetching in it. Plus, Jesse seemed to adore her in blue, making her wonder if he favored the color.

Alas, the moment she attempted to tie on the sash, her insides heaved in protest.

Mercy! She dashed for their bedroom window, threw it open, and leaned her head outside, gagging. Since her stomach was empty, nothing came up, thankfully. A cool morning breeze swirled around her face, providing immediate comfort, though it was several minutes before she dared to stand upright again. As a precaution, she kept the window open, allowing the breeze to fill the room.

With a wistful look at the lovely sash, she finally opted to leave it off. It was a tremendous sacrifice of vanity, because the dress looked incomplete without it. However, it seemed wise to avoid putting anything constricting around her waist at the moment. Hopefully, the strange feelings would soon pass. She'd heard about this condition before. Some women referred to it as morning sickness. Her only comfort was that it was temporary.

Hers seemed to be passing, so she deemed herself ready to go in search of her husband. Leaving their bedchamber, she stepped gingerly down the hallway. A clatter of dishes pulled her toward the kitchen. Perhaps she could catch Jesse hauling in a fresh pail of milk. Drawing in shallow breaths of air, in the hopes of avoiding another bout of morning sickness, she all but tiptoed her way into the kitchen.

Mr. Crocker glanced up when she stepped through the doorway. "Morning, Mrs. Hawling! I hope you ain't creeping around like a ghost on my account. I've been up for ages."

"A good morning to you, too, sir." She gave him the briefest of curtsies, bending her legs only and trying not to put any undo pressure on her stomach.

"What's the matter, lass?" He scrutinized her features. "You're lookin' a little puny around the edges."

She moved farther into the room, not certain how to answer his question. She preferred for Jesse to be the first to hear her news. "You don't happen to have any tea I can brew?" It was the first time since she'd left New York that she truly longed for something she'd left behind.

He nodded at a pot on the stove. "I do, but I have a fresh pot of coffee already made up."

She shook her head, knowing how black and thick he made it. She was unable to bear the thought of sipping something so potent and bitter. "If it's all the same to you, I'd rather boil up some water and indulge in a cup of tea, instead."

"Suit yourself." He nodded at the empty silver teapot resting on the cabinet.

She hurried forward to snatch it up. She'd always been fond of her teas — every flavor from cinnamon to orange to jasmine. Back when he was alive, her father had seen to it that their home was stocked with the finest imports from around the globe. It was a memory that had her blinking back tears.

"You sure you ain't fallin' ill?" Mr. Crocker demanded as she puttered her way to the stove.

"I certainly hope not." She forced a bit of cheer into her voice that she didn't truly feel. "There's no time for that, is there?"

"Nope. There never is, lass."

Trying to keep her voice casual, she inquired. "Have you seen Jesse this morning?"

His gaze narrowed. "I was about to ask you the same thing. That infernal cowboy did all my chores and done took off without his breakfast."

Alarm filled Iris's mouth at the thought that her uncle's hired cronies might've finally caught up with her husband.

"Never fear, lass. Took his badge and horse with 'em. Went to tend to some deputy business, I reckon."

"How long?" she muttered beneath her breath.

"How long fer what?" he demanded.

She hadn't intended for him to hear her whispered expulsion. "How long do we have to live in fear like this?" she sighed. "I don't know about you, but every moment I worry about those thugs returning. Don't you?"

He nodded at his loaded rifle and cane resting against the wall. "So long as I keep my trusty iron partner handy, I figure anyone who comes sniffin' around has more to worry about than me."

She mustered a wobbly smile, knowing he was trying to make her feel better. "I cannot thank you enough for all you've done for Jesse and me. We've been so happy here, sir." Her voice hitched, despite her effort to keep her emotions under control. "I don't want it to end." She couldn't bear the thought of leaving his homestead. Ever.

"Now, now, lass," he soothed. "That man of yourn 'll be back in no time, and everything 'll be right as rain again. You'll see."

No sooner did Iris get a pot of tea brewed, did a clatter of horses' hooves make them dash for the back porch.

Despite hobbling on a cane, Mr. Crocker deliberately elbowed his way in front of her. "Hold my cane, and stay back," he ordered tersely as they reached the corner of the veranda. He leaned against the wall for support as he raised his rifle.

Unable to stand meekly in wait, Iris peeked around his elbow. Two horsemen were riding their way up the packed dirt driveway, churning up a small cloud of dust with their hooves.

As the riders galloped closer, Mr. Crocker pulled the trigger and fired a warning shot over their heads.

The horses veered apart and careened in opposite directions, one flying past them on either side of the house.

As Mr. Crocker reloaded, Iris recognized the man on the horse nearest them. She grabbed his shoulder. "Don't shoot!" she cried. "They're Jesse's brothers!" Why had they ridden with such haste to the farm, and where was her husband? Panic filled her throat at the possibilities that flew to mind.

It took several minutes for Jonah and Jack to calm their horses and ride back into view. Even more alarming were the number of rifles strapped over their shoulders.

Jonah was the first to leap from his horse. A broad-shouldered bear of a man, he beckoned wildly at her to approach. Unlike his brothers, who always had on Stetsons, he was wearing a raccoon skin cap. He'd also replaced his usual denim work trousers and shirt with a deerskin tunic and leggings. There was something singularly ominous about his appearance.

Forcing her trembling legs to move, Iris hurried down the side porch steps. "Where is Jesse?" she cried.

"On his way." Jonah bent to cup his hands, motioning for her to climb onto Jack's horse. The seriousness of his expression was no comfort.

"But I'm not even in my riding habit," she protested. She'd be forced to ride side saddle. Again.

He didn't answer. He simply hefted her up behind Jack.

"Hold on." Jack turned his head sideways to ensure she was ready.

"Where are we going?" She glanced desperately back at Old Man Crocker, who looked oddly unsurprised by what was taking place. *What aren't you men telling me?*

"You'll be payin' a visit to our neighbors, lass," Mr. Crocker informed her with a faint smile that didn't reach his eyes. "Been meanin' to introduce ya to 'em."

Neighbors, as in...oh! She caught her lower lip between her teeth, realizing he must be referring to the wild band of Comanches that were supposedly embedded in the mountains to the east of his homestead.

"What about Jesse?" Her voice shook.

"Like Jonah said, he'll be joining us shortly." Concern was etched deeply into the lines of Jack's aquiline features. "I'm gonna need you to hold on tight."

"Go easy, please," she ordered softly, realizing it was time to let at least one person know about her condition. "I have reason to think I am with child."

"Great balls of fire," he muttered beneath his breath. He raised his reins and took off at a walk. Moments later, he hugged his horse into a gentle trot.

❧

EDWARD DOGGED JESSE'S HEELS AS HE STALKED ACROSS THE rear porch of the jailhouse. "I'm telling you, Fargus Hildebrand's thugs are back in town. Or maybe they never left. Who knows? Either way, you should be heading in the opposite direction. Back to Iris, where you belong."

"I need to see my father." Jesse plowed stubbornly ahead, digging for his keys to unlock the rear door of the jailhouse, where the prisoner cells were housed.

"It can wait," Edward insisted. He slapped a hand against the wall, making Jesse glance up.

"No. It can't." Jesse had waited a long time for the truth. It was now or never, since there was a good chance he'd be in hiding for a good while after today. "Why are you here, anyway? You told me what you came to tell me. You can go now." He'd never seen Edward this disheveled. His normally well-pressed white shirt was wrinkled and dusty, as if he hadn't changed since yesterday, and his Stetson was askew.

"Not on your life," the innkeeper growled. "If you're fool enough to remain exposed like this, I reckon you'll be needing someone to watch your back."

Jesse unlocked the door and pushed it open. "I didn't ask for your help."

"Well, you're getting it anyway. You're as stubborn as a donkey. You realize that, right?" Edward's pistol was already in his hand. He spun around, facing the open doorway. "Hurry up, before you get us both killed."

"Well, look what the wind blew in!" the senior Mr. Hawling drawled from behind the shadowy bars of his cell. His mirth abruptly disappeared when he caught sight of Jesse's face.

"The truth, father. Now!" Jesse slapped both hands against the bars.

"What are you talking about—?"

"Once and for all, did or did not Ike Remington cheat in cards?" Jesse grated out.

"You can't be serious," Edward snarled from the doorway. "We're about to have a pair of outlaws gunning us down, and you're still worried about the ownership of my blasted inn?" He whipped his second pistol from its holster and aimed it at the doorway. "By all that is great and good, if that fool piece of real estate means that much to you and your brothers, I'll draw up a deed and we'll split the ownership fifty-fifty. Won't do any of us a bit of good, though, if we don't come out of here alive."

Jesse glanced in irritation over his shoulder, feeling the first tendrils of shame. "If I want your input, I'll ask for it."

"There's no need to give away what you rightfully own, lad." Mr. Hawling expelled a long-suffering gust of air. "As much as it pains me to admit it, your grandfather bought the property free and clear."

Jesse gripped the bars of the jail cell harder. "Then why in tarnation did you lead us to believe otherwise all these years?"

"Because the truth is worse." Though his father spoke quietly, he might as well have been yelling because of the import his words carried. "I figured it was better for you to hate a dead man than it was to know what really happened." Even inside the shadowy prison cell, Jesse could see how pale his father had grown.

"Tell me," he begged. "All of it."

"If you insist, son, but don't say I didn't warn you. The truth is, your ma was never quite right after that drunken assault outside the General Store. She snatched up one of my revolvers while I was sleeping and rode into town looking for the fella that did it."

Please, no. Jesse braced himself for the worst.

"I followed her, but I was too late. She'd already found him and put a bullet clean through his chest. It was on the road leading to Christmas Mountain Inn and I was preparing to hide the body, but Old Ike had to ruin everything by riding in our direction on his confounded wagon. As it turns out, he'd ridden into town to bail his intoxicated clerk out of jail. Caught me red-handed before I could finish the deed. The old geezer quickly sized up what had happened, but he had the decency to help me concoct a new story. At his suggestion, I bloodied up the nose of our corpse. Then he awoke his fool clerk, so he could supposedly witness me murdering the bloke in cold blood."

So you're innocent. Just as Jesse had suspected all along. Well, maybe not quite what he'd expected. His father was a blasted hero.

Jesse pressed his face against the bars of his father's cell, struggling not to weep. So great was his misery, it was a wonder the cold metal didn't start to sizzle.

"Given the same set of circumstances, I'd do the same thing all over again." Mr. Hawling gripped the bars, bringing their foreheads together. "She was worth it, Jesse. Your ma was worth it. In the end, justice was served. The only kind I was able to live with, at any rate."

Jesse knew the rest of the story. His mother had never fully recovered from the assault on her person. "When did she—?" he choked.

"Old Man Crocker rode past on his way back from a milk delivery at the inn. He took her to his farm so his wife could tend to her. She only lasted a few more days. I never saw her again, but I assure you, she died knowing how much I loved her."

Jesse knew the rest of the story, how he and his brothers had fended for themselves as teens and every day since. Angry tears dripped down his face. "You're innocent," he muttered. "I always knew it."

Mr. Hawling shrugged. "A crime was committed, and someone had to pay. Like I said, she was worth it, son. Just like that new wife of yours is worth it. Like Edward said, you'd best be getting back to her. If you got trouble headed your way, your place is at her side. Not mine."

"Thank you!" Edward snapped from the other side of the narrow room. "Finally a Hawling who can talk sense!"

Jesse pushed back a few inches to stare at his father through damp eyes. "How did you know I was married?"

Mr. Hawling grinned. "It's a small town. Word travels fast."

Right. By way of Old Man Crocker.

"They're coming," Edward snarled. "Probably saw your horse tethered out front."

"Who's coming?" Mr. Hawling demanded, growing serious again.

"Long story." And Jesse wasn't in the mood to tell it. His heart was too heavy from his tragic discoveries. "The short version is, my wife is an heiress, someone robbed her blind, and now they want us both dead."

"They'll be upon us in one, two, three!" Edward counted down the seconds until the first dark shadow fell across the doorway of the jailhouse, blocking the morning sunlight.

Jesse spun around, but didn't recognize the intruder, a man whose features were mostly hidden beneath the brim of his Stetson and the black cloth tied over the lower half of his face. The intent of the revolvers in his hands, however, was clear.

He reached for his own pistols, but his father was quicker. Lunging against the bars, he whipped both guns from his son's holsters. "Move!" he roared.

The weaponless Jesse dropped to one knee in the nick of time. The first shot narrowly missed Edward's shoulder, but the bullet embedded itself solidly in the would-be assailant's chest. He lurched back a step before crumpling to the plank floor with a stunned look on his face. By some miracle, neither of his guns discharged on his way down.

Only a half second later, the footfalls of his partner could be heard. Before his shadow fully bloomed in the doorway, Mr. Hawling fired again. This time, his bullet flew between the chinks in the log wall, shooting straight through the dried mud filler.

There was an answering *oof* on the other side of the wall. Edward flew through the doorway, guns aimed to fire, with Jesse right behind him. They found a second outlaw on his knees, clutching a bloody arm. Mr. Hawling's bullet had hit home, though this one wasn't fatal.

It was like the past repeating itself all over again. They had a dead man on their hands, just like his father had so many years ago. Jesse and Edward traded a harsh look as Jesse slapped the thug's hands in cuffs.

"I witnessed it all." Edward's jaw was hard. "I'll testify to the truth of what happened here today."

"Do whatever you think is best." Jesse was already striding across the porch. "I have to get to Iris. Lord only knows how many more thugs her uncle will be sending her way."

"Wait!" There was so much urgency in Edward's voice that Jesse paused and glanced back.

The innkeeper was holding out one of his pistols to Jesse, the butt carefully pointed downward.

"Thanks." Jesse stepped closer to accept the gift. "I am officially in your debt too many times over to count."

"No. You're not. That's what friends are for."

Something hard and brittle, that had encased Jesse's heart for as long as he could remember, finally shattered. "I reckon that's what we are, isn't it?"

Edward nodded. His sweat had long since turned the dust on his cheeks to muddy rivulets, but the grimy streaks in no way hid his elation. "It's what I've been trying to tell you." His dark eyes glinted with mischief. "That is, if you can ever forgive me for failing to marry your wife."

Jesse chuckled. "I'll consider it."

"And I'll see to it that your pa doesn't take the rap for what went down here. It was self defense."

Jesse nodded, no longer able to speak past the enormous lump of gratitude in his throat. He spun around and jogged for his horse, knowing he and Edward Remington had likely crossed paths for the last time. Though Jesse was thankful they weren't parting as mortal enemies, he still wasn't willing to risk Iris's safety in the hopes of winning a court case.

This was goodbye. They both knew it.

CHAPTER 10: FAREWELLS
EDWARD

Just as the hoofbeats of Jesse's horse were fading, Sheriff Rick Dawson came skidding around the side of the porch. Both his badge and the revolver in his hands glinted like silver fire in the morning sunlight.

"I was down the street a ways, but I came as soon as I heard the shots." He was panting as if he'd run the entire way. "Wish I'd been closer, but you know how windy ol' Mav can get down at the General Store. Was down there grabbing my order of gunpowder, and—" He stopped short at the sight of the two bodies on the ground, one motionless and the other writhing in agony from his gunshot wound. "What in the blazes happened here?"

Edward shrugged, forcing his expression to one of indifference. "These two bandits attacked Jesse while he was visiting with his father. To their grave misfortune, his father fired back."

"How in tarnation did Mr. Hawling get his hands on a gun?" Sheriff Dawson's expression turned ferocious.

Because Jesse trusted his father a little too much. Probably because he'd known all along the man was innocent, utterly blameless for the crime he was serving a life sentence for.

"It appears Jesse might've been standing a little too close to his father's cell." Edward hated making Jesse look bad, but it was better than having yet another Hawling falsely accused of a crime he didn't commit. Besides, there was a good chance Jesse was in the wind for good, in which case it almost didn't matter what his boss thought of his actions.

The sheriff made a scoffing sound. "Amateur," he muttered. "That's exactly why I had no interest in taking on a new deputy. Takes forever to get 'em trained up. Then the big cities recruit 'em right away from you."

Edward was relieved to note he didn't sound too put out by Jesse's misstep with their longest standing prisoner. He nudged their newest prisoner with the toe of his boot, eliciting a loud groan from him. "This fellow here is about to 'fess up to exactly what happened, detail by blessed detail."

The man spat at Edwards' boots. "Ain't telling you nothin'!" he howled.

"That's alright." Edward mocked. "As the Lord is my witness, I'm happy to inform the sheriff of your attempted murder of Jesse Hawling and the accidental homicide that resulted when his father fired back in self defense. I sure hope Fargus Hildebrand is paying your heirs enough to make it worth your while to hang from a noose."

At the mention of Iris's uncle, their prisoner jolted in surprise.

It was the very reaction Edward had been hoping for, verifying his suspicions that Iris's uncle was ultimately behind the attack. "So what's it going to be?" He reached down to yank the man's mask below his mouth. "The truth? Or were you planning on single-handedly going down for the crimes of a filthy rich man?" He nodded at the thug's dead partner.

"Looks like there's no one else left to share the blame, if you don't start talking."

At the man's stubborn silence, he prodded. "For what it's worth, there's a silly rumor making its way around this part of the country." He winked at Rick Dawson behind the man's head. "Something about the Christmas Mountain sheriff having a soft spot in his heart for men who find the courage to tell the truth."

"Alright, alright." The man's mouth twisted bitterly, telling Edward that he'd hit just the right chord with him. A paid mercenary was loyal to one thing only — his paycheck, which this particular fellow wouldn't be receiving since he'd been caught. Edward had thrown the thug the one lifeline he had left, the hope of staying alive by cooperating with the law.

❧

WEARINESS JANGLED THROUGH EVERY BONE IN EDWARD'S body by the time he rode his horse back to the Christmas Mountain Inn. An extremely harried Lacey met him at the front door with her chubby nephew on one hip.

"Where have you been?" She looked as weary as he did, bless her heart! There were splatters across the front of her pink summer frock, as if she'd been sprayed by water. He wondered if she'd recently given Malachi a bath.

"Helping defend Jesse from a pair of outlaws." He yawned and reached for the lad. "It's quite a story. How long do you have?" he teased, knowing she would insist on hearing every last word of it.

To his surprise, she burst into tears. "Jesse's still alive?" she choked. "I was so worried when he came tearing through here earlier on his horse. Whatever he said to his brothers sent all three of them galloping off together. I've been running the inn alone for the past several hours. I'm at my wits' end, sweetheart!"

Edward's shoulders slumped. Things were far worse than he feared, if all the Hawlings had high-tailed it away from the inn. Had Fargus Hildebrand sent even more mercenaries after Iris, then? As badly as Edward wanted to head straight for Old Man Crocker's farm to offer his assistance, there was no way on heaven or earth he'd leave his wife and son alone to fend for themselves. He could hardly believe the Hawlings had seen fit to leave them alone this long, as it was. Then again, they'd probably assumed he was present when they'd left.

A rumble of horses' hooves from behind him made him pivot to face the long, winding path leading to the inn. *What now?* To his relief, it was Mav Peterson, rattling their way in his work wagon. A second man was riding beside him. As they drove closer, Edward's chest constricted with recognition.

His father, Penn Remington, was the man sitting beside Mav. His tall, thin figure was ramrod straight and his expression as hard as flint. He didn't wait for Mav to completely stop the wagon before hopping to the ground.

"I suppose you think you've won," he announced coldly. His black suit was dusty from his ride, but he carried himself as if he was wearing a king's robe spun of pure gold threads.

"Here," Lacey reached for Malachi, "I should probably take him inside." She searched her husband's face. "Are you going to be alright out here alone with him?" she whispered.

"Yes. Just stay inside until it's over, love." Edward's earlier exhaustion faded beneath a surge of indignation. It was the second time his father had shown up at their inn, unannounced.

"Hello, Father." He knew this was neither a family visit

nor a social call. His sire was solely here to represent Fargus Hildebrand's twisted financial interests.

Mav parked the wagon and leaned his elbows on the faded knees of his overalls. "I reckon this fellow is who he says he is, eh? Looked too much like you for me to doubt his claim that he was your pa. Said he needed a ride to the inn, so I offered to oblige." His cheery smile faded. "For a fee, of course."

With his nose wrinkling in distaste, Penn Remington dug for his wallet. He tossed a few coins in Mav's general direction, not waiting to see if he caught them.

"So this is what it's come to?" Edward folded his arms, more ashamed of his father than he'd ever imagined possible. "Stealing from women and defending the guilty? My, how far the mighty have fallen!"

His father's thin lips twisted in anger. "If you think for one second, a judge will take the testimony of a thug over that of an upright member of society, you are sorely mistaken, son."

Edward shrugged, refusing to rise to the bait. "You're welcome to take your chances in court. Of course, there will also be the eyewitness testimonies of a sheriff, his deputy, and me." He paused for dramatic effect. "A licensed attorney, law-abiding citizen, and innkeeper. I'm not sure if that counts in your book as an upright member of society, but I think it'll count in the books of every Texas judge around." He forced a smile. "In the event you've forgotten, you're no longer in New York."

Mav nimbly hopped down from his wagon to collect the coins Penn Remington had so rudely tossed his way. Then he proceeded to tether his horses. "I'll head inside to check on the Misses." He trudged heavily up the stairs. "Figure she might could use a hand in the midst of all this ruckus."

"Appreciate that, Mav." Edward was more grateful than

words could express for the man's show of neighborly kindness. He'd be sure to thank the General Store owner more properly at a later date.

"Think nothin' of it," Mav returned with an offhand wave. Then he pushed open the door of the inn and went in search of Lacey.

"I am well aware I've left the civilized world," Penn Remington noted sarcastically. "I guess I shouldn't be surprised your unstable former fiancée chose to hide out here."

"Hide?" Edward's brows shot up. "Is that what Fargus Hildebrand is claiming? Because I have an asylum employee who stands ready to claim otherwise," he bluffed. "In case you were unaware, Iris Hildebrand was assaulted, drugged, and kidnapped from her home." That part was true, at least.

His father's expression twisted with glee. "You're not, by any chance, referring to Miranda Jennings? The same employee who was let go from her job for losing track of a patient en route to the asylum?"

"I reckon you'll find out when we go to court." Edward refused to be intimidated. His father was wrong on every level, and they both knew it. "You can either take your chances that the wheels of justice will roll in the favor of your client, who is a heinous criminal.. Or..." he taunted, pausing to let his father mentally fill in the blanks of what he left unsaid.

The silence dragged on between them for several seconds. Interestingly enough, Penn Remington was the first to break it. "Or what, son?"

"Or you can advise Fargus Hildebrand to do the right thing by his niece, open up a local bank account, and start paying her the monthly allowance she's due." Edward was heavily improvising, at this juncture, but he didn't care. His own refusal to marry Iris had set off the current train of events. He owed it to Jesse to do what he could to put a stop to the mayhem before matters spun completely out of control.

"Or," his father countered again, "I can continue with my current lawsuit and prove Iris is mentally unstable and that her rogue of a husband, who served a stint of his own in the same asylum, is equally unfit to manage her fortune."

"You can try." Edward unfolded his arms and half turned away from his father to indicate he was preparing to head indoors. "As I've already stated, I'm well prepared to defend my clients from such heinous accusations. I don't expect it will take much effort for the judge to appoint an unbiased medical expert to assess their mental faculties. So if you persist in backing a criminal instead of doing what is right, I will see you in court." He turned away and reached for the stair railing, lifting his boot to the first step.

"Wait." His father's voice was carefully controlled. "Are you suggesting that this entire court case will go away if my client reinstates Iris Hildebrand's monthly allowance?"

Without turning around, Edward spoke in an equally unemotional tone. "She's married now. Her legal name is Iris Hawling." He ascended another stair. "Oh, and make sure the account is located at the Christmas Mountain Bank."

"What about her mansion in New York?"

Her mansion, eh? Hers and not that of his filthy client. Edward kept walking, knowing he'd won, though he paused at the front door of his inn. "My recommendation would be to liquidate it, since my client has no plans to return east." He twisted the doorknob and left his father staring after him.

Mav Peterson met him in the doorway of the kitchen. He had a damp towel in one hand and one of Jack's aprons dangling loosely around his neck. He was far too rotund to wrap it around his middle and tie it properly. "What's this I hear about a falling out between you and the Hawlings?"

Edward was only half listening. "It depends," he drawled. "Why don't you first tell me what you heard, and I'll verify the parts that are true?" *If any*. Mav Peterson was notorious for repeating and spreading gossip, much of which wasn't entirely accurate.

Mav blinked owlishly at him. "Word has it that the Hawlings have quit working for you and joined up with that new enterprise Old Man Crocker has going on with the Comanches."

Again, Edward had no earthly idea what the man was referring to, though he intended to find out. Pronto!

"I'm sorry, my friend. I can neither confirm nor deny the rumors at this time. What I can tell you is that the Hawling brothers still reside in my carriage house, but they had to leave work early today to handle a pressing family matter." He pushed past the open-mouthed General Store owner to glance around the kitchen. "Where's my wife?"

"Crying her eyes out in the library, that's where!" Mav muttered. "Ain't every day a woman loses her entire staff in one fell swoop. She's fit to be tied." He shook his head. "If you'd like, I can spread the word that you're looking to hire more staff."

Edward nodded, feeling his tiredness return. "That would be great, Mav. I've been toying with the notion of expanding my staff for some time now." Fortunately, Mav could spread factual announcements every bit as quickly as gossip. He was like a human megaphone.

MAV REMAINED AT THE INN THROUGH THE DINNER HOUR, helping with the cooking and serving. Penn Remington stoically joined the Christmas Mountain Inn guests in the dining room. He ate in silence, didn't offer to pay for his meal, and Edward didn't ask him to. He did, however, corner Mav again in the kitchen, when he left the room to refill a pitcher of fresh-squeezed lemonade.

"What would it take to get you to stay the night?" He and Lacey had two sets of guests on site besides his father. One was a retired couple on their way north to visit their children in Oklahoma, and the other was a trio of ranchers from a few towns over. They were looking to expand their herds by purchasing longhorns from some of the locals. Edward would certainly welcome Mav's help overnight, if he were willing.

"I tell you what." Mav finished wiping down the kitchen cabinets. It was past dinnertime, and their guests' bellies were full. "I've been thinking on it all afternoon, and I might have a solution to your problem, at least a temporary one."

"I'm all ears," Edward returned dryly, bracing himself for a dubious proposal.

"Indeed, it was something I overheard Clink Redwood fussing about the other day while he was in the store. Apparently, he has a mail-order bride arriving in town on the evening train, and none of his prospective grooms are fully paid up on their contracts. His problem, not yours. At any rate, he needs a place to put her up for the night. What if you were to arrange for her to work off her room and board?"

It wasn't the worst idea Edward had ever heard. "You don't, by any chance, know what skills this young woman happens to possess?"

Mav shrugged his burly shoulders, as if Edward's question was of little consequence. "She's a woman, Ed. I reckon she can cook and keep a clean house. Ain't those the minimum requirements for a mail-order bride?"

Edward wasn't aware of any "minimum requirements," but he let Mav's comment slide. He was too desperate for help to be overly picky. "What will it cost me to keep you here a bit longer, at least? No more than an hour or two. I need a man with a rifle keeping an eye on Lacey and Malachi, while I run an important errand. And I'd be happy to take the wagon and collect Clink's mail-order bride on my return trip."

"If you can make it back by nightfall, we'll call it even." Mav's smile was one of pure satisfaction, making Edward wonder if he'd been biding his time all afternoon to introduce this very topic. He dearly loved to butt in to other folks' business, though his heart was generally on the right side of things. "Folks in town have been looking after each other for decades. That's just what we do."

"I appreciate it, Mav. Would you like for me to return my father to town, as well, or would you rather take him back yourself and earn another fee?"

"I reckon that's for him to decide." Mav's bushy brows shot upward. "Just so you know, he was making noises on the way here about reserving a room and staying a spell."

As if Lacey and I need one more thing to worry about. "In that case, I'm going to need you to keep an eye on him in my absence." Edward didn't trust his father enough to leave him unattended under the same roof as Lacey and Malachi.

Mav looked sympathetic. "I gathered there might be some hard feelings between the two of you."

Edward resisted the urge to roll his eyes, knowing Mav was always overjoyed to get his thick fingers on another juicy piece of gossip. "Just keep your eye on him. Please." He'd warn Lacey to do the same, but she was already well aware of the need to proceed with caution around his parents.

THE EVENING SUN WAS JUST STARTING TO DIP ON THE horizon when Edward drove up the heavily rutted road leading to the Crocker farm.

Jonah rushed out the front door to greet him, then stopped short. "I thought you were the doctor."

Edward couldn't help noticing that Jonah dropped the "boss" or "sir" he normally used when addressing him, which he enormously appreciated. He'd been trying for months to get the oldest Hawling brother to drop the ridiculously unnecessary formalities between them. "Why?" He parked the wagon, secured his horse, and leaped to the ground. "Is Jesse hurt?" Hurrying up the porch stairs, he entered the home without knocking.

"No. It's ah..."

A pitiful sight met him. Old Man Crocker was sprawled on the sofa, looking so feeble that Edward paused in alarm. "What happened, sir?"

"Old age." Mr. Crocker gave a wheezing cackle and tried, without success, to sit up. "I already done lasted longer than the odds had me pegged fer."

"Are you ill, sir?" Edward hurried across the sparsely furnished living room to drop to a knee beside the aging farmer.

"Just tired." There was an odd rattle to his breathing that Edward didn't like.

He glanced over his shoulder at Jonah, who was watching them grimly with his thick arms crossed. "Are either of you gentlemen going to tell me where Jesse is?"

Jonah gave him a slight head shake. "Jack went to fetch the doctor. If you'll come with me for a quick minute, Edward, there's something in the other room I could use your help with."

Hoping he had news about his missing youngest brother and wife, Edward followed him.

Jonah led him down the hall to the library before turning to face him. "Jesse and Iris are gone. To where, I have no idea. They didn't leave a forwarding address. If you could spare Old

Man Crocker the news on his deathbed, however, I'd be much obliged. He's come to think of them like the son and daughter he never had."

Gone? Deathbed? Edward's stomach started to hurt. "Did either Jesse or Iris drop any hints about where they might be going?" he asked dully. It was exactly as he'd feared. Jesse was a mountain man at heart. He wasn't waiting for the slow wheels of justice to turn. He intended to remain a free man, even if it meant going on the run.

"If only I could've gotten here sooner," he muttered when Jonah didn't immediately answer, "but my father showed up at the inn, threatening more legalities. I negotiated as hard as I could. If things go as I advised, Iris's uncle will be opening an account in her name and reinstating her monthly allowance. Immediately."

Jonah's jaw dropped. "You did all that for Jesse and the woman you refused to marry?" He sounded so amazed that it made Edward sad.

"Of course I did!" He was astounded at the Hawlings' persistence in viewing him as the enemy. "You're my trusted employees."

Jonah glanced away. "Not anymore, sir. I'm sorry, but we won't be coming back to work at the inn."

And we're back to formal titles. "Why?" Edward suddenly felt ten years older.

"I'm not at liberty to say, sir." Jonah looked sheepish but resolute.

"Very well. What can I do to help out here, before I head back home?" Edward was still very much aware they had a dying man in the next room.

Jonah shrugged. "I dunno. You're the attorney. Maybe ask Old Man Crocker what his last wishes are?"

"I can do that." Edward didn't know what it was going to

take to get the Hawling brothers to trust him, but he sure intended to keep trying.

"I'll rejoin you in a bit." Jonah held back, making Edward wonder if he possessed some sort of superstitious fear of death.

Edward made his way back to Mr. Crocker's side. "How are you feeling, sir?" He squatted down beside the sofa again.

"Like I'm on my last leg." The older gentleman tried to chuckle, but it ended up coming out as an alarming wheeze.

"Jonah tells me that Jack has gone to fetch a doctor. Is there anything I can do for you in the meantime? I was a lawyer before I became an innkeeper, so if you have any last wishes..."

"A lawyer, you say?" Mr. Crocker's dull gaze sharpened. "You don't reckon it's too late to write me up a will, eh?"

"Not at all. I just need a pen and paper."

Mr. Crocker raised a trembly hand and pointed with one bony finger. "In the desk, over in the corner."

Nodding, Edward rose to fetch the requested items. After a moment's hesitation, he ended up carrying the small desk and chair across the room. He set them down beside the sofa and took a seat. Uncapping the inkwell, he dipped Mr. Crocker's pen. "You may begin, sir."

"I ain't never had no children of my own, so I'd like to leave all my earthly possessions to Jesse Hawling and his brothers, split evenly. Their pa was a good friend. Don't care much for what happened to him. Maybe this'll right a few old wrongs." His mildly accusing stare wasn't lost on Edward, but he didn't figure a deathbed was the proper place to set anyone straight on a situation like that. Besides, he fully approved of Mr. Crocker's decision for how to handle his last will and testament.

He asked the old farmer a few questions about the number of structures on his property, so he could list them one by one. He also inquired about the quantity of livestock on the premises and the amount of acreage he owned.

"Is there a legal deed to the place?" He signed his name to the bottom of the page as the author of the document.

"Shore is. There's a loose stone on the fireplace. You'll find the deed behind it."

Edward nodded and nudged the document he'd written in Mr. Crocker's direction. "If you'll just sign here, sir." He hastened to stand behind the fellow. Reaching beneath his too-thin arms, he gingerly helped raise him to a sitting position. Mr. Crocker's signature turned out shaky but legible.

"You're not half as bad as I heard," the farmer mumbled as Edward helped him lie down again on the sofa.

Indeed? Edward raised one eyebrow. "Well, that certainly tickles my curiosity. What have you heard?"

"Nothin' good, which clearly ain't true." The older gentleman offered him a faint smile. "That infernal feud between the Remingtons and the Hawlings started a long time ago. You young-uns just happened to inherit it."

Edward was more puzzled than ever. It was clear that Mr. Crocker believed the yarn that Ike Remington had spread at the senior Mr. Hawling's bidding. It was a dead shame, since it wasn't true. Not a lick of it!

"Well, I don't plan to keep it going," Edward announced flatly. "I have nothing but a good opinion of Jonah, Jack, and Jesse. Well, mostly. Jesse can be something of a hothead, but that's just his way. You don't mind his temper so much after you get to know him."

"But you must!" Mr. Crocker's rasping cough took way too long to recover from this time.

"What do you mean, sir?" Edward firmly clasped his wrinkled hand, wishing there was more he could do beyond writing up his last will and testament.

"You hafta help keep the feud goin'. Let everyone think

that Jesse and Iris have fled town, and the Hawlings blame the Remingtons for it. It's the only way to keep her fool guardian from sending more bounty hunters after her."

"I sure wish there was a better solution to the problem." Edward was surprised at how well informed the aging farmer was for a person who wasn't supposed to even know that Jesse and Iris were missing.

"Well, there ain't. And Jesse's going to need all the help he can get, protectin' his bride while she's in the family way." Mr. Crocker lapsed into another fit of coughing.

Iris is pregnant? All Edward could do was gape at that startling announcement. No wonder Jesse was going to such extremes to protect her. He couldn't blame the man one bit, because he'd be doing the same for Lacey if their roles were reversed. No one should trust Penn Remington and Fargus Hildebrand for one simple reason; they weren't trustworthy.

"I'll protect Jesse and Iris's secrets, Mr. Crocker. I'll protect them at all costs," Edward promised.

When there was no answer, he glanced across the sofa at the feeble farmer, only to discover his eyelids were closed. The rise and fall of his chest had ceased. He was gone.

Moments later, he heard Jonah return to the room. "Is it over?" he asked hoarsely.

"Not quite." Edward pointed at the will that was still drying on the man's desk. "I recorded his last wishes. You're going to need to read it. Then find your brothers and read it to them, as well."

Perhaps Mr. Crocker's last will and testament would serve as the catalyst to bring Jesse out of hiding someday. The blasted cowboy had always wanted to be a wealthy man, and now he finally was.

It was way too bad he didn't know it.

EPILOGUE

Eight months later

Iris rose early, before her infant son awoke, and stepped outside her cavern home. It was a chilly mountain morning, so she kept the deerskin cloak Chief Pecos had gifted her wrapped tightly around her shoulders.

He'd been so kind to allow her and Jesse to stay on his reservation throughout her lying in. They owed him a debt of gratitude they might never be able to repay.

Strong arms enclosed her from behind and pulled her against a solid male chest. "Good morning, Mrs. Hawling." Jesse's warm mouth found a sensitive spot on her neck, eliciting a giggle at the way his beard tickled the soft skin there.

"I love that sound." He reached up to palm her cheek and brought her mouth to his.

"Is that the only part of me you love?" she teased. "My laugh and nothing else?"

He spun her around in his arms, pretending to scowl in concentration. "I'll have to think on the matter a bit. Maybe I can get back to you later with my answer?"

"No, you may not." She stood on her tiptoes to slide her arms around his neck. "I want to hear it now." The increased thump of his heartbeat against hers gave lie to his words. Nearly a year after their marriage, he was still as affected by her nearness as she was by his.

"Demanding wench." He swooped in for another kiss, taking his time and rendering her breathless. "That should clear things up for you."

"I still want to hear the words, Jesse," she pleaded. He didn't consider himself to be an eloquent speaker, so all too often he held back for fear of not being able to impress his high-born wife.

His dark eyes started to twinkle. "Do you remember how I once told you I'd lasso the moon and stars for you, if you'd but ask?"

"I do," she murmured dreamily.

"Well, this is probably as close as I'll ever get to that." He reached inside the pocket of his deerskin trousers and produced a delicate gold band. The diamond resting in the center of it caught the sun and flashed like a prism of fire.

It was a ring. "For me?" Iris gasped.

"No. It's for my other wife." He smirked. "Of course it's for you, darlin'!" Without waiting for a response, he slid it on her fourth finger. "I'm sorry it's a year late, but it took me a while to save up for it."

She beheld him with tearful pride, knowing how much money they had piled up in the bank from the monthly allowance her uncle paid them. But it was just like Jesse to ignore that fact. She knew what he meant by "saving up." He'd earned every penny to purchase her gorgeous diamond by the sweat of his brow. And for that reason, the ring was all the more precious to her.

"Jesse," she sighed. "Just when I was wondering if it was possible to love you more!"

"Well?" He gave her a comical look, pretending confusion. "Did you ever figure it out?"

"I did." She cupped his face in her hands, adoring the scrape of his beard against her bare fingers. He'd grown a short beard throughout the winter, as black and wavy as his head of hair. "My love for you just keeps growing. So much that I was half afraid there wouldn't be any left for our son when he was born."

"I reckon I can allow you to share a small part of your heart with Little John," her husband conceded with one of his cockiest grins, "so long as you always save the biggest part of it for his pa."

"Always and forever," she promised softly, leaning closer to brush her lips against his.

CHIEF PECOS TURNED AWAY FROM THEM ON A DISTANT hill, wondering what a gem of a woman like Iris had ever seen in a stubborn rogue like Jesse Hawling. The cowboy was relentlessly hardworking, but he possessed the temper of a rattlesnake when anyone crossed him. In fact, the only person who seemed to be able to gentle him was his wife. In her arms, he was like a lump of damp clay, malleable and almost human.

Rather like himself lately. The chief glanced up at the sky, gauging the time of morning. In another half hour, he'd be riding to the Christmas Mountain Inn to deliver their morning supply of fresh milk to a certain dark-haired beauty who served in their kitchen.

A chief delivering milk. That's what this woman had reduced him to. A mere delivery boy. His comrades were probably chuckling up their sleeves at his weakness.

Meg Chastain. The name was far too plain to do her

justice. He'd never understood the ways of white men. A woman like Meg deserved to be called something far more enchanting like Two Dark Moons. That's what he'd been secretly calling her since the first day she'd caressed him with her magical brown eyes. There was no stoic Native blood in her. The woman's eyes seemed to reflect every emotion she felt. They could sparkle with mirth one moment and crackle with righteous indignation the next. She was more enchanting to watch in action than a gathering storm.

Alas, she barely noticed his existence. His fault, of course. He was always rendered speechless in her presence. A pity, because there were a thousand things he would like to say to her and another thousand places he'd like to show her, if they ever graduated to speaking terms.

"Chief Pecos." A teenage lad named Night Flyer approached him with a wooden bucket in hand. Inside was the fresh milk he pulled each morning from one of their milk cows. Unlike the elders in their tribe, he wasn't all that skilled at hiding his youthful smirk. "Would you like me to make this morning's delivery for you?"

It was the same question he asked every morning, the ornery lad. He asked it, just to be amused all over again by his chief's insistence on delivering the pail of milk himself.

Ignoring the question, Pecos held out his hand. "I'll take it. There's wood to be chopped and horse stalls to be mucked."

At the disappointed cast to the teen's face, he added, "And Sanko could use some help in the ring." Sanko was their top horse trainer. He was so successful in saddle breaking wild horses that the other men in their tribe were convinced he had a magical way of communicating with the creatures.

Pecos knew better, though. What Sanko had was patience and perseverance. He never gave up, no matter how bleak things looked. Pecos had learned that lesson from him. It was the reason he returned day after day after day to Meg Chastain's kitchen, if only to woo her with his eyes.

He mounted his horse, bareback, and made the short, two-mile trip to the Christmas Mountain Inn. It was fascinating to him how prosperous the town had become since the innkeeper's arrival. Nearly every business downtown had a fresh coat of paint and some sort of addition, including Mav's General Store. The ranches to the south were booming as well, though their increase in prosperity wasn't as visible. They were breeding and selling more head of cattle than ever. Plus, the Hawlings had made quite a name for themselves, showing and selling the Comanche mustangs. Folks came from all over to purchase the once-wild creatures.

The only negative, whatsoever, about the fast-growing mountain town was the fact that it had divided itself into two distinct parts — the Remingtons in the north and the Hawlings in the south. And from that division, a fierce rivalry had evolved. When rodeo season rolled around, the citizens on the north sat on one side, while the citizens on the south sat on the other. The rivalry in itself wasn't so bad; the culture that accompanied it, however, was less savory. Bawdy jokes arose from one side of town about the other and vice versa. Sometimes, the jibes grew so sharp that fisticuffs broke out. So, despite the prosperity that accompanied the changes in Christmas Mountain, there were times when Pecos found himself preferring the way things used to be — before the arrival of the Remingtons and Hawlings.

With one big exception, however, in the form of Two Dark Moons.

Riding around to the side entrance of the inn kitchen, Pecos waited patiently for the object of his interest to make her appearance. She usually kept him waiting for a minute or two. Today, however, three minutes passed, then four, then five.

Only when a breathy moan met his ears did he slide off his stallion.

"Two Dark Moons," he called in worry. Then he inwardly upbraided himself for calling her by his made-up name for her. "Meg," he corrected. *No. That's not right, either.* His white friends had a thousand rules of conduct that he never seemed to be able to keep straight. Among them was the fact that a man did not call a woman by her given name until expressly requested to do so. Instead, she was addressed as a "Miss" in front of her surname. Miss Chastain, in her case.

"Pecos?" she gasped. "Is that you?"

"I am here." He reached the kitchen door and pressed his ear to it. Was she ill or injured?

"The door is unlocked. I'm going to need you to—"

He was already pushing it open and striding inside, where he found her sitting in the middle of the kitchen floor. She was white-faced and clutching her ankle.

"What happened?" He didn't hesitate to stride forward and crouch before her.

"I'm such a fool," she moaned. Her normally warm and welcoming gaze was glazed with pain. "Instead of running to fetch the ladder, I cheated and tried to stand on top of a cane chair to reach a top shelf, and..." She broke off her self-recriminatory tirade with an *oomph* of misery as he brushed her hands aside.

Though it was hard to tell with the way her high-heeled boots were laced, her ankle was so swollen that he feared it was broken.

He fumbled with the ridiculously tight laces without success, only eliciting more bleats and puffs of pain from the woman he was trying to impress.

In a burst of sheer desperation, he reached for the blade he kept sheathed at his side and cut straight through the black leather of her boot.

This time, Miss Chastain's gasp was one of sheer horror. "Oh, Pecos!" she cried. "What have you done? They're the only shoes I own."

"I'll buy you another pair," he snarled.

As he'd feared, the bone was broken.

"Here." He reached without looking to the cabinet directly above them in search of the nearest kitchen utensil. It turned out to be a wooden spoon. *Perfect*. He handed it to her. "Bite down on this." There was no time to waste. He had a broken bone to set.

Meg clenched the spoon handle between her pearly white teeth.

"Are you ready?" he inquired huskily.

She nodded, as pale as the bucket of milk he'd left outside.

He pressed both thumbs in quick succession against the fractured bone to set it in place.

She gave a keening wail around the spoon but managed to remain sitting upright. He'd seen grown men pass out from less.

"The worst is over," he soothed. He stood and looked around her tidy work space, liking how clean the kitchen was and how good it smelled — like a curious mix of freshly baked bread, apples, and spices. Seconds later, he found what he was looking for, a clean white linen towel.

Returning to Meg's side, he stooped in front of her and held out a hand for the spoon. Their fingers brushed as she returned it. Holding her gaze, he neatly spliced the long handle into two neat splints with his blade. Swiftly whittling the ends to remove the sharp edges, he pressed the pieces against either side of her ankle to hold the fractured bone straight. Then he wrapped it securely with the white cloth and tucked the end in place.

"You'll need to prop it up to reduce the swelling."

Without thinking, Pecos lifted her in his arms, preparing to carry her wherever she directed. There was no way she could continue working in the kitchen in her current state.

"The man speaks." Though pale, Meg gripped his shoulders like a lifeline. "I've often wondered if you even possess a voice."

"I do," he returned gruffly, liking the way she was holding on to him. She possessed a strength that belied her delicate build. *I just can't seem to locate it in your presence, precious.*

"Then how come you've never spoken to me before?"

"Where should I take you?" he countered, not knowing how to answer her question.

"To the front parlor," she supplied quickly. "I'm on duty, so I'll simply rest a bit, then get back to work."

"You work here?" He teased, knowing it was a foolish question. His only purpose was to keep her talking. He wanted to know more about the enchanting woman. Who she was and where she came from. And even more importantly, where she was going next.

"Of course I do, you silly man!" she chided. "In a manner of speaking. The mail-order bride agency owner hasn't found me a husband yet, so he made an agreement with the Remingtons to let me work here to cover my room and board until he does."

Pecos was startled to hear of the difficulty in finding Meg Chastain a husband. It seemed particularly odd, considering how many unwed men were living on the mountain. Hundreds, maybe even a few thousand. His surprise was accompanied by dismay at the realization she would most likely be wed soon.

"What kind of groom is the owner of your agency seeking for you?"

"A wealthy one, I reckon." Meg gave a wry chuckle. "I'm not privy to all the details, but I suspect he keeps raising my price. Either that, or the Remingtons are paying him to keep me single. I think they like the work I do here at the inn so much that they aren't anxious to lose me to marriage."

"How much?" he demanded curtly.

She shook her head at him, bemused. "I was just teasing about that other stuff. I truly don't know, Pecos. Why do you ask?" The pain in her gaze faded into the most alluring sparkle, while her cheeks blossomed to a rosy pink.

Pecos stared for a moment, hardly able to believe that all he needed to do was produce a sum of money, and this enchanting woman would be his. The supreme foolishness of his neighbors on Christmas Mountain was about to become his good fortune.

"Why?" He met and held her gaze. "Because I intend to pay it."

"ARE WE EVER GOING TO MOVE BACK TO THE CROCKER farm?" Iris mused, as the red and gold rays of dawn streaked across the sky.

"Would you care to, darlin'?"

"I'm undecided." She and Jesse stood wrapped in each other's arms, watching the mountains light up around them. It was her favorite part of the morning, one he always tried to be back in time to be a part of.

He always rose early to help Sanko and Night Flyer with the horses, but he usually returned to their stony castle for breakfast. That's how Iris thought of their Comanche home.

She and Jesse had been living with the tribe for the better part of a year now, and had earned their place in the majestic caverns overlooking the Christmas Mountains. It simply wasn't possible to have a home with a more regal view, nor was Iris all that interested in raising their son in a town that was fast being divided into the Remingtons versus the Hawlings.

A day never went by that she didn't feel some measure of guilt in the part she'd played in the deepening divisions between the north and south sides of Christmas Mountain. Then again, one never knew when her creepy uncle would send his next pair of mercenaries to hunt her down and do away with her for good.

As long as the legend of her and Jesse's infamous disappearance continued on, and as long as the south continued to persecute the north over it, she and Jesse could raise Little John in peace. For now, it was enough. It had to be enough.

As the dawn glinted to a full blast, Iris gasped in delight. Never in all her days would she grow tired of watching the sunrise with her gallant savior.

"I love you, Jesse," she breathed. "I love you so much that my heart can hardly contain it."

"I love you more." He claimed her lips to seal his promise, and the morning glinted even brighter from behind her closed lids.

Her heart sang over the miracles they'd found together on the mountain — love, peace, and more happiness than she'd ever dreamed possible. Maybe if she prayed hard enough, their miracles would eventually spill over to the rest of Christmas Mountain. It was a town that could certainly stand to see a few more miracles.

Someday.

Want to find out how Chief Pecos is planning to win the heart of the most sought after mail-order bride in town? Start reading
Bride for the Tribal Chief
today!

SNEAK PREVIEW: BRIDE FOR THE TRIBAL CHIEF

A *mail-order bride who desperately needs the protection of a husband, a tribal chief who thinks he's the perfect solution to all her troubles, and the lineup of hopeful rivals who plan to give him a run for his money...*

Chief Pecos is far from thrilled by the sudden influx of new settlers to Christmas Mountain. He prefers things to continue as they've been for centuries with his tribe, taming and riding the mustang herds that roam the foothills. Until a mail-order bride steps off the train with a price on her lovely head... All of a sudden, he can think of one good exception to the way things have always been.

Meg Chastain actually has more than one price on her head — first, a bounty for a crime she didn't commit; and, secondly, a bridal contract fee that her penny-pinching matchmaker keeps raising. Oh, and she's fairly certain her new employers at the Christmas Mountain Inn are pressuring the bridal agency to delay her placement, since their customers have never been happier with the meals she so graciously stirs up each day.

With a group of bounty hunters closing in, a whole line of hopeful grooms vying for her hand in marriage, and one dark and handsome tribal chief who seems to be silently courting her during his daily visits to the inn, will Meg succeed in finding her perfect match before it's too late?

Grab your copy of
Bride for the Tribal Chief
Available in eBook and paperback on Amazon + FREE in Kindle Unlimited!

ABOUT THE AUTHOR

Jovie Grace is an Amazon bestselling author of sweet and inspirational historical romance books full of faith, hope, love, and cowboys. She also writes sweet contemporary romance as Jo Grafford.

1.) Follow on Amazon!
https://www.amazon.com/author/joviegrace

2.) Join Cuppa Jo Readers!
https://www.facebook.com/groups/CuppaJoReaders

3.) Follow on Bookbub!
https://www.bookbub.com/authors/jovie-grace

4.) Follow on Facebook!
https://www.facebook.com/JovieGraceBooks

SNEAK PEEK: ELIZABETH

Early November, 1866

Elizabeth Byrd rubbed icy hands up and down her arms beneath her threadbare navy wool cloak as she gingerly hopped down from the stagecoach. It was so much colder in northern Texas than it had been in Georgia. She gazed around her at the hard-packed earthen streets, scored by the ruts of many wagon wheels. They probably would have been soft and muddy if it weren't for the brisk winds swirling above them. Instead, they were stiff with cold and covered in a layer of frost that glinted like rosy crystals beneath the setting sun.

Plain, saltbox buildings of weathered gray planks hovered over the streets like watchful sentinels, as faded and tattered as the handful of citizens scurrying past — women in faded gingham dresses and bonnets along with a half-dozen or so men in work clothes and dusty top hats. More than likely, they were in a hurry to get home, since it was fast approaching the dinner hour. Her stomach rumbled out a

BRIDE FOR THE DEPUTY

contentious reminder at how long it had been since her own last meal.

So this was Cowboy Creek.

At least I'll fit in. She glanced ruefully down at her workaday brown dress and the scuffed toes of her boots. Perhaps, wearing the castoffs of her former maid, Lucy, wasn't the most brilliant idea she'd ever come up with. However, it was the only plan she'd been able to conjure up on such short notice. A young woman traveling alone couldn't be too careful these days. For her own safety, she'd wanted to attract as little attention as possible during her long journey west. It had worked. Few folks had given her more than a cursory glance the entire trip, leaving her plenty of time to silently berate herself for accepting the challenge of her dear friend, Caroline, to change her stars by becoming a mail-order bride like she and a few other friends had done the previous Christmas.

"Thanks to the war, there's nothing left for us here in Atlanta, love. You know it, and I know it," Caroline had chided gently. Then she'd leaned in to embrace her tenderly. "I know you miss him. We all do." She was referring to Elizabeth's fiancé who'd perished in battle. "But he would want you to go on and keep living. That means dusting off your broken heart and finding a man to marry while you're still young enough to have a family of your own."

She and her friends were in their early twenties, practically rusticating on the shelf in the eyes of those who'd once comprised the social elite in Atlanta. They were confirmed spinsters, yesterday's news, has-beens...

Well, only Elizabeth was now. Her friends had proven to be more adventurous than she was. They'd responded to the advert a year earlier, journeyed nearly all the way across the continent, and were now happily married.

Or so they claimed. Elizabeth was still skeptical about the notion of agreeing to marry a man she'd never met. However,

Caroline's latest letter had been full of nothing but praise about the successful matches she and their friends had made.

Be assured, dearest, that there are still scads of marriageable men lined up and waiting for you in Cowboy Creek. All you have to do is pack your bags and hop on a train. We cannot wait to see you again!

Caroline had been the one to discover this startling opportunity by reading an advert in The Western Gentlemen's Gazette. It had been placed there by a businessman who claimed to be running the fastest growing mail-order bride company in the west.

All I had to do is pack my bags and leave behind everyone and everything I've ever known to take part in the same opportunity. Elizabeth shivered and pulled her cloak more tightly around her. Attempting to duck her chin farther down inside the collar, she wondered if she'd just made the biggest mistake of her life. She was in Cowboy Creek several days later than she'd originally agreed to arrive, having wrestled like the dickens with her better judgment to make up her mind to join her friends.

Oh, how she missed the three of them! Caroline, Daphne, and Violet were former debutantes from Atlanta, like herself. All were from impoverished families whose properties and bank accounts had been devastated by the war. It was the only reason Elizabeth had been willing to even consider the foolish idea of joining them. She was fast running out of options. Her widowed mother was barely keeping food on the table for her three younger sisters.

Even so, it had been a last-minute decision, one she'd made too late to begin any correspondence with her intended groom. She didn't even know the man's name, only that he would be waiting for her in Cowboy Creek when her stage-coach rolled into town. Or so Caroline had promised.

With a sigh of resignation, Elizabeth reached down to grasp the handles of her two travel bags that the stage driver had unloaded for her. The rest of her belongings would arrive in the coming days. There'd been too many trunks to bring along by stage. In the meantime, she hoped and prayed she was doing the right thing for her loved ones. At worst, her reluctant decision to leave home meant one less mouth for Mama to feed. At best, she might claw her way back to some modicum of social significance and be in the position to help her family in some way. Some day...

Her hopes in that regard plummeted the second she laid eyes on the two men in the wagon rumbling in her direction. It was a rickety vehicle with no overhead covering. It creaked and groaned with each turn of its wheels, a problem that might have easily been solved with a squirt of oil. Then again, the heavily patched trousers of both men indicated they were as poor as church mice. More than likely, they didn't possess any extra coin for oil.

Of all the rotten luck! She bit her lower lip. *I'm about to marry a man as poor as myself.* So much for her hopes of improving her lot in life enough to send money home to Mama and the girls!

The driver slowed his team, a pair of red-brown geldings. They were much lovelier than the rattle-trap they were pulling. "Elizabeth Byrd, I presume?" he inquired in a rich baritone that was neither unpleasant nor overly warm and welcoming.

Her insides froze to a block of ice. This time, it wasn't because of the frigid temperatures of northern Texas. She recognized that face, that voice; and with them, came a flood of heart wrenching emotions.

"You!" she exclaimed. Her travel bags slid from her nerveless fingers to the ground once more. A hand flew to her heart, as she relived the sickening dread all over again that she'd experienced at the Battle of James Island. She was the unlucky nurse who'd delivered the message to Captain David Pemberton that his wife had passed during childbirth. The babe hadn't survived, either. But what, in heaven's name, was the tragic officer doing so far from home? Unless she was mistaken, his family was from the Ft. Sumpter area.

"Nurse Byrd." The captain handed his reins to the man sitting next to him, a grizzled older fellow who was dressed in a well-pressed brown suit, though both knees bore patches. "We meet again." He offered her a two-fingered salute and reached for her travel bags. He was even more handsome than she remembered, despite the well-worn Stetson shading his piercing bourbon eyes. During their last encounter, he'd been clean shaven. His light brown sideburns now traveled down to a shortly clipped beard. If the offbeat rhythm of her heart was any indication, he wore the more rugged look rather nicely.

Which was neither here nor there. Elizabeth gave herself a mental shake. She'd been searching for a sign, anything that would shed light on whether she was doing the right thing by coming to Cowboy Creek. Encountering this man, of all people, only a handful of minutes after her arrival, seemed a pretty clear indication of just how horrible a mistake she'd made.

She nudged the handles of her bags with the toe of her boot to put them out of reach. "Y-you don't have to go through with this, captain. I can only imagine how difficult it is for you to lay eyes on me again." If it was anything close to how difficult it was for her to lay eyes on him, it would behoove them both to take off running in opposite directions. "I am quite happy to board with one of my friends until I can secure passage back to Georgia." The whole trip had been a horrible miscalculation of judgment. She could see that now as she stared stonily into the face of the officer who'd led the man to whom she was once affianced into the battle that had claimed his life. Captain Pemberton didn't know that wretched fact, of course. How could he? They were neither personally, nor closely, acquainted at the time.

The expression in his eyes softened a few degrees as he regarded her. "I gather you found the young man you were searching for during the war?" he noted quietly. "Otherwise, you would not be here."

Preparing to marry you, you mean! "I found him, yes." Her voice was tight with cold and misery. It was all she could do to keep her teeth from chattering. "I found him and buried him."

"Ah." He nodded sadly. "Words are never adequate in situations like these. Nevertheless, I am deeply sorry for your loss."

His regret appeared genuine. She sensed he was a kind man, a good man, despite the deplorable circumstances under which they'd made their first acquaintance. *More's the pity!* Though she couldn't exactly hold the captain responsible for the Union bullet that had taken her Charley's life, she couldn't just up and marry the man responsible for leading him into harm's way, either. Could she?

Perhaps it was the cold breeze numbing her brain, but suddenly she was no longer certain about a good number of things.

"Come, Elizabeth." The commanding note in David Pemberton's voice brooked no further arguments. "You must be famished after such a long journey, and you'll catch your death out here if we linger in the cold."

This time, Elizabeth's toes were too icy to function when he reached for her travel bags. She stood there shivering while he tossed them inside his wagon. She was both shocked and grateful when he proceeded to unbutton his overcoat and slide it around her shoulders.

It was toasty warm from his body heat and smelled

woodsy and masculine. "I th-thank y-you." She was no longer able to hide how badly her teeth were chattering.

"Think nothing of it, Miss Byrd." He slid a protective arm around her shoulders and guided her on down the street. "A friendly fellow named Frederick owns the eatery next door. Since our wedding isn't for another two hours, how about we head over there for a spell? We can grab a bite to eat and thaw out at the same time."

Our wedding? Her lips parted in protest, but she was shivering too hard to form any words.

As if sensing her confusion, he smiled and leaned closer to speak directly in her ear. His breath warmed her chilly lobe and sent a shot of...something straight down to her toes. "Surely an angel of mercy like yourself can spare the time to swap a few war stories with an old soldier?"

She clamped her teeth together. *An angel of mercy, indeed!* She'd felt more like an angel of death back there on the battlefield. There were days she lost more soldiers than the ones she managed to save. It was something she preferred never to think of again, much less discuss.

"If I cannot make you smile at least once in the next two hours, I'll purchase your passage back to Atlanta, myself," he teased, tightening his arm around her shoulders.

Now *that* was an offer she couldn't afford to pass up. She didn't currently possess the coin for a return trip, though she had to wonder if the shabbily dressed captain was any better for the funds, himself.

She gave him a tight-lipped nod and allowed him to lead her inside the eatery.

The tantalizing aromas of fresh-baked bread, hot cider, and some other delectable entrée assailed them, making her mouth water. A pine tree graced one corner of the dining area. Its boughs were weighed down with festive gingerbread ornaments and countless strands of red ribbon. A man in a white apron, whom she could only presume was Captain Pemberton's friend, Frederick, cut between a line of tables and hurried in their direction, arms outstretched. "You rebel you! Someone might have at least warned me you were one of the lucky fellers gittin' himself a new wife."

"Oh-h!" Elizabeth's voice came out as a warble of alarm as, from the corner of her eye, she watched a young serving woman heading their way from the opposite direction. She was bearing a tray with a tall cake and holding it in such a manner that she couldn't see over the top of it. She was very much at risk of running in to someone or something.

David Pemberton glanced down at her concern, but all she could do was wave her hand in the direction of the calamity about to take place.

His gaze swiftly followed where she pointed, just in time to watch the unfortunate server and her cake collide with Frederick. White icing and peach preserves flew everywhere. His hair and one side of his face were plastered with a layer of sticky whiteness.

The woman gave a strangled shriek and slid to her knees. A puppy dashed out of nowhere and began to lick the remains of the gooey fluff from her fingers.

Afterwards, Elizabeth would blame it on the long journey for frazzling her nerves to such an extent; because, otherwise, there was no excuse on heaven or earth for what she did next.

She laughed — hysterically! It was ill-mannered of her, unladylike to the extreme, and completely uncalled for, but she couldn't help it. She laughed until there were tears in her eyes.

Captain Pemberton grinned in unholy glee at her. There was such a delicious glint in his whiskey eyes that it made her knees tremble.

"A deal's a deal, nurse; and the way I see it, you did more than smile. You laughed, which means I'll not be needing to purchase that trip back to Atlanta for you, after all. Unless you've any further objections, we've a little less than two hours before we say our vows." He arched one dark brow at her in challenge.

Their gazes clashed, and the world beneath her shifted. As a woman of her word, she suddenly couldn't come up with any more reasons — not a blessed one — why they couldn't or shouldn't get married.

Tonight!

Read the whole story today!

Elizabeth

The whole trilogy is available in eBook, paperback, and Kindle Unlimited on Amazon.

SNEAK PREVIEW: HOT-TEMPERED HANNAH

BOOK #1 IN THE MAIL ORDER BRIDES RESCUE SERIES

A *bounty hunter is on the trail of a missing mail-order bride who looks identical to the only woman he's ever loved.*

When Gabe Donovan is recruited to track down a missing mail-order bride, he receives the shock of his life. She could pass as a twin to Hannah Merrill, the partner he thought he lost in a fire — the same woman he never got around to confessing his feelings to, for fear of ruining their partnership. If she's still alive, though, it means she must have faked her death to start over fresh some place else. Leaving him precious little time to track down the missing beauty before the past she's been running from finally catches up to her, and he loses her again...this time for good!

Heartwarming historical romance with a dash of humor, a twist of intrigue, and a happily-ever-after! Each title in this series can be read as a standalone.

Start reading
Hot-Tempered Hannah
today.
(Psst! It's a complete 12-book series, so you can binge read them all!)

ACKNOWLEDGMENTS

Many thanks to my editor and friend, Cathleen Weaver, for her incredible insight and eye for detail. I'm also very appreciative of my amazing beta readers, Mahasani and Debbie Turner. Plus, I want to give a shout-out to my Cuppa Jo Readers on Facebook for reading and loving my books!

JOVIE'S TITLES

Mail Order Brides of Christmas Mountain Series

Bride for the Innkeeper

Bride for the Deputy

Bride for the Tribal Chief

Brides of Cedar Falls

Lawfully Witnessed

Wanted Bounty Hunter

The Bounty Hunter's Sister

Rescuing the Blacksmith

Wild Rose Summer

Mail Order Brides on the Run Series

Cowboy for Annabelle

Cowboy for Penelope

Cowboy for Eliza Jane

Mail Order Brides Rescue Series

Hot-Tempered Hannah

Cold-Feet Callie

Fiery Felicity

Misunderstood Meg

Dare-Devil Daisy

Outrageous Olivia

For a printable list of my books:

Tap here

or go to:

https://www.jografford.com/joviegracebooks

For a printable list of my Jo Grafford books
(sweet contemporary books)

Tap here

or go to:

https://www.JoGrafford.com/books

Made in the USA
Middletown, DE
04 November 2024